SOFT TARGETS

SOFT TARGETS

BENJAMIN INKS

DOUBLE‡DAGGER

— www.doubledagger.ca —

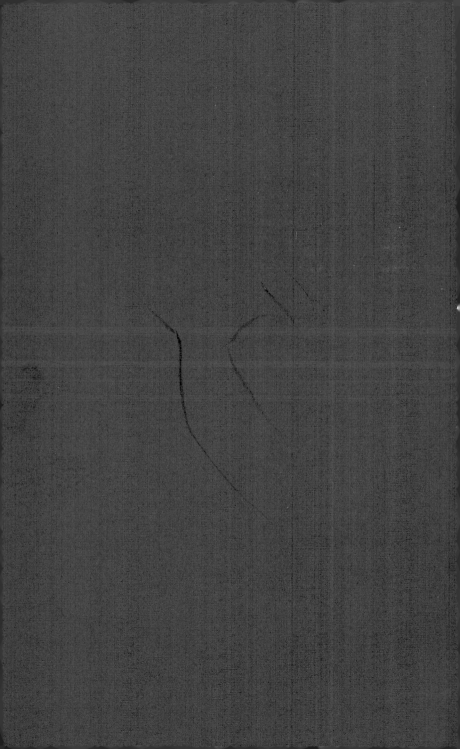

Stay

*This book is dedicated
to the wild men and women of the
1-91 CAV.*

Library and Archives Canada Cataloguing in Publication
Inks, Benjamin author
Soft Targets / Benjamin Inks

Issued in print and electronic formats.

ISBN: 978-1-990644-54-2 (soft cover)
ISBN: 978-1-990644-56-6 (e-pub)
ISBN: 978-1-990644-59-7(Kindle)

Editor: Phil Halton
Cover design: Pablo Javier Herrera
Interior design: Winston A. Prescott

Double Dagger Books Ltd
Toronto, Ontario, Canada

www.doubledagger.ca

Table of Contents

Part 1

Part 2

Part 3

Military Terminology

ACU: Army Combat Uniform
ANA: Afghan National Army
AO: Area of Operations
ARCOM: The Army Commendation Medal
BDU: Battle Dress Uniform
CIB: Combat Infantryman Badge
CLS: Combat Lifesaver (medical training)
COP: Combat Outpost
EOD: Explosive Ordinance Disposal
ERB: Enlisted Record Brief (career history report)
EXFIL: Exfiltration (extraction)
FNG: Fucking New Guy (disparaging epithet)
FOB: Forward Operating Base
Hooch: Slang for troop living space, often comfortable plywood rooms
    with AC and bunk beds
IED: Improvised Explosive Device
KIA: Killed in Action
MK. 19: An automatic grenade launcher
MOS: Military Occupational Specialty
MRAP: Mine Resistant Ambush Protected
NCO: Non-Commissioned Officer
OEF: Operation Enduring Freedom
OP: Observation Post
PFC: Private First Class
POG: Person other than Grunt (disparaging epithet)
PT: Physical Training (usually conducted in the early morning)
QRF: Quick Reaction Force
REMF: Rear Echelon Mother Fucker (disparaging epithet)
ROE: Rules of Engagement
RPG: Rocket Propelled Grenade
SGT: Sergeant
SF: Special Forces
SFC: Sergeant First Class
SSG: Staff Sergeant
SOP: Standard Operating Procedures
TBI: Traumatic Brain Injury
TOC: Tactical Operations Center
VBIED: Vehicle Borne IED
WIA: Wounded in Action
XO: Executive Officer

I would like to thank the many editorial teams who selected the following stories for publication.

"On a Mountain in Logar" first appeared in *Proud to Be: Writing by American Warriors Volume 10.*

"Jack Fleming Lives" first appeared in *The Wrath-Bearing Tree.*

"Learning to Be You" first appeared in *Line of Advance.*

"Love in the Time of Combat Injuries" first appeared in *Military Experience & the Arts.*

&

"Honeycombs" first appeared in *Proud to Be: Writing by American Warriors Volume 11.*

To the extent that boys are drawn to war, it may be less out of an interest in violence than a longing for the kind of maturity and respect that often come with it.

~ Sebastian Junger, *Tribe*

Everyone serves the good wine first, and when people have drunk freely, then the poor wine. But you have kept the good wine until now.

~ John 2:10

BLOOD WINGS

THERE IS NOTHING MORE AGONIZING than the transitory stages of military service. The mind can make a heaven of hell and vice versa, but I'd argue only purgatory is true suffering. When you're eighteen and alone in the barracks with nothing but fantasies to keep you occupied, you begin to crave pain if only to distract yourself from sheer idleness; from nothingness. Such was my mind before Airborne School at Fort Benning, Georgia.

I had just graduated the fourteen-week training course to become a bonafide infantryman. I was now a *something*, and the drill sergeants were no longer cruel. I was a private, yes, but a private with purpose. A unit had claimed me: an airborne unit! And during that in-between week that felt like a year, I would often stare up at the sky and imagine myself floating with tactical grace. I'd earn those Jump Wings soon enough. And other badges, too. Air Assault Badge. Then a *Raaanger* Tab. I'd go through Special Forces selection and then become a sapper. Halo Badge. Diving Badge. Motherfucking Spaceman Badge. I'd earn them all. My uniform would be as decked out as a Mideast dictator.

My ambition was endless, but my world was small. Very small. In fact, I spent that holdover week in the same mold-infested barracks I'd suffered the last four months in. Good God, I was ready for a change. And just as I was planning on cutting my fingernails and arranging the clippings into interesting shapes, Drill Sergeant Shrader, proud owner of the Army's most-coveted mustache, shouted from down the hall: "Clifton, pack your crap and get your ass across post. You're going to Airborne School."

I immediately dumped the wall locker they had taught us to keep so neat and *dress-right-dress*. All my rolled-up socks, clean ACUs, and standard-issue underwear became a big ball I ramrodded into my duffle, turning it into a big green punching bag. Racing down the hallway, I paused at Drill Sergeant Shrader's office.

The drill sergeants ordered us to write an introduction letter on arrival, a brief wave of civility before an endless storm of tyranny. I had made the embarrassing mistake of closing my letter with *Your brother in arms*, and Shrader never let me forget it.

Why if it isn't Clifton—my brother in arms! he would shout at every encounter before making me do something painful, tedious, or unnecessary.

Stopping at his door one last time, he turned to me, twirling the golden ferret on his lip. It was probably non-regulation facial hair, but no superior officer would dare command him to shave it: that would be like shooting a bald eagle off a mountain ledge.

He approached grinning and actually shook my hand. "You better get those wings, Private. And they better be *bloody*."

"Yes, Drill Sergeant." I said mechanically. I'd probably said *yes, Drill Sergeant* 50,000 times since my arrival.

Descending the barracks and stepping into a sweltering post-morning Georgia, Shrader yelled out the window: "Always lock your knees before landing, Private."

And I said it. Dear God, I said it.

"Yes, Drill Sergeant!"

My grandparents raised me on a cattle farm in Montana, my parents absent for reasons I'd rather not discuss. The days were long and the chores enjoyable. No time to be idle, *no hurry up and wait* like the Army, just *hurry up and hurry up*. I relished working hard and earning my keep with two rugged geezers who were declining in their later age. Like the livestock we kept, I sometimes felt they were raising me healthy but behind a corral where I could do no damage or break their tender hearts by running away. Coming home after signing enlistment papers crushed them.

"Matthew Thomas Clifton!" grandma cried, uncertain whether to be angry or crestfallen.

"I have to do this while you two can run the farm without me," I said, hoping to soften the blow by suggesting the Army was just a phase. By the end they were convinced I was embarking on four years of self-discovery. *Just like college*, I proposed. Grandpa signed off on the Army easy enough: "Go get it out of your system, bud. And then come back, ya' hear?"

They firmly believed I'd return to carry on their legacy.

Me? I thought so too. Though after becoming an infantryman—I was having doubts.

A gleaming white shuttle bus took me across Fort Benning, from Sand Hill to airborne country. The trip was smooth and air-conditioned. The bus driver was pot-bellied and told me in his whistling southern accent to "Climb aboard, young man." As I did, I felt a warm exhilaration pass through me, like a convict exiting a supermax prison. I was entering a new autonomous world, free from the dehumanizing supervision of Drill Sergeants. I could go anywhere, within reason. I could do anything, within reason. I could buy candy; see a movie; gorge myself at a pizza buffet. And then the shuttle bus rounded the corner and those beautiful training towers rose in the distance, the backdrop of a two-mile jogging track.

We would soon be leaping out of those towers during the second week of Airborne School. The swath of a track, two-miles drawn in an imperfect circle, was hallowed ground we would soon be shuffling on—in boots—to build up enough strength in our knees and ankles to survive the impact of parachuting. After seeing all this, I wanted one thing. Forget the personal freedom and junk food, I wanted my damn Parachutist Badge.

I could already picture graduation: the Black Hat instructors carefully aligning the small metal pin above the *A* of my U.S. Army nametape. Coarse hands delicately pushing the sharp tines ceremoniously into my uniform, a brief grin from the Black Hat before pushing harder, past the cotton of my undershirt and into my skin where blood from my chest would stain my shirt and fuse hard-earned badge to the flesh of hard-assed private. *Blood Wings.* Fuck yeah! But how had this hazing ritual come to be? And who in their right mind would want this?

Me. That's who.

Rites of passage have existed since time immemorial—and still do in certain parts of the world. In modern America, regulated to impotence with rules and policies and elitist morals, few opportunities to challenge oneself remain. Indeed, the all-volunteer military might be the last proving ground for adolescents entering adulthood. In this hierarchical organization, where individuality is stripped away and replaced by a single uniform, most recruits strive to differentiate themselves from the herd.

I was always going to volunteer for Airborne School, to

stand apart from those who did not—*dirty, nasty legs.* Just as I will demand my Blood Wings, to stand out from an even more select crowd. There will be no official paperwork detailing this commendation, yet that makes it more enticing. *He did it not for another shallow praise on his ERB but for the sheer experience of it. Stone-cold son of a bitch.*

Standing in line at airborne HQ, waiting to turn my name into a three-digit roster number, I'd never felt like more of a badass.

"Hey, you," a Black Hat seated at a processing table singled me out, his hand pointing like a knife.

My voice cracked. "Me, Sergeant Airborne?"

"Yes, *you*, you gummy-bear-lookin' motherfucker. Split this line and come get your roster number."

Self-conscious of my wide ears, I resisted the urge to rub my scalp where dark, fuzzy hair was sprouting after fourteen-weeks of a constant buzz cut. I hopped to his table, and Sergeant Airborne Palmer, who spoke through two pouches of Skoal Wintergreen, christened me airborne candidate 326.

Before dismissing me, Palmer examined my nametape against a clipboard.

"Clifton. You're one of Drill Sergeant Shrader's."

"Yes, Sergeant Airborne."

"Shrader said you'd be coming by. Said to make you feel *extra welcome* here at Jump School."

This did not bode well.

He produced an opened can of Skoal. Held it out to me like offering a breath mint. The scent alone—of fresh gum minced with brown goop—was enough to green my gills.

"You dip, Airborne?"

It was promising that he referred to me as 'Airborne' and not 'Private.' Not wanting to come across as the inexperienced youth I was, I went to pluck one of the soggy pouches.

"Git your little-girl fingers out of my face," he said,

withdrawing the tobacco.

I knew I should have clipped my nails.

He chuckled under his breath and then told me in so many words to exit his building. I obeyed, his tobacco-coated voice shouting behind, "Neeext."

It was the damnedest thing. I couldn't tell if it had been a negative interaction or a positive one.

Ground Week

There was an illusion at Airborne School that rank did not matter. That we were all there to become paratroopers and everyone from a major to a buck private received the same treatment. This felt true at times: lining up behind a staff sergeant to perform a parachute landing fall for the hundredth time; being served the same meal as the captain behind you; watching a rotund 2nd lieutenant fail the fitness exam and be sent back to his unit without Jump Wings, *ouch*.

Other times, the divisions of rank were subtly reintroduced. This was most evident with the carefree attitude of the cadets, recruits who enjoyed a nebulous standing in the military ecosystem. Some came from military academies such as West Point and were about as gung-ho as I was but with an air of playful superiority. Other cadets were contracted ROTC and acted like civilians. It wasn't their prospective college degree that gave them such leeway, they just hadn't been broken down to the same level of desperate conformity. They were being groomed as leaders, not followers. They didn't stand in parade rest for the Black Hats, and they seemed to get away with it, too. I would have loved to see these kids, who were only a few years older than me, spend a week in Sand Hill. To watch Drill Sergeant Shrader rip the weird polygonal rank off their chest and scream clever insults at them, his beautiful mustache close enough to tickle their cowering brows.

But after each day of Airborne School ended, we split into our respective factions to embrace our off-duty identities. The female cadets shed the drab ACU uniform for bright, tight-fitting designer clothes, letting their hair tumble out of regulation buns. As they walked by their perfume turned me calm and stupid, as if critical regions of the brain had just been swabbed with a numbing agent. It had been far too long since I'd seen anyone so delightfully feminine.

Barnes, a private like me, and an Animal Care Specialist of all MOSs, suggested taking a cab to a strip club. Little did I know there are no fewer than four strip clubs close to Benning, and we were about to embark on either another rite of passage or a misinformed cliché. Barnes had a habit of contorting his lips and pinching his chin when in thought. He had this calm, deliberate way about him. During the fitness exam the Black Hat grading his pushups said he wasn't going down far enough. His count went from twenty to zero, but Barnes just kept pumping them out, unfazed, this time his chest and face smacking the pavement with each repetition. He's the only guy I know who did fifty-eight pushups to qualify for Jump School. I learned, in-between lap dances (sorry, Grandma), that he came from Columbus, Ohio, not to be confused with Columbus, Georgia—home of Fort Benning. He wouldn't shut up about the illustrious Ohio State Buckeyes and the degree he planned on earning after the military.

"Don't you want to go to school somewhere else?" I asked, practically shouting over a Rihanna song. "Somewhere besides your hometown?"

He grew up so close to that damn university, went to football games, and participated in its culture, it's all he'd ever wanted since high school.

"I almost went Infantry, like you," he said.

"Yeah, why didn't you?"

"My uncle was drafted for Vietnam. He said if I pick Infantry, he'll save me the trouble and shoot me himself. Said I need an MOS with a future in the civilian world."

"So . . . animals?"

"I like animals."

"Well, who doesn't? But what about the glory of combat? What about the experience of doing something risky and noble and bold?"

"I'm here, aren't I?"

And it's true, he was. In two weeks he would be jumping out of a perfectly good airplane the same as me. Barnes said nothing after that. Sipped his Coke thoughtfully as if it were a refreshing, cold beer.

I sipped my soda, too. Suddenly our gauche environment no longer interested me. All I could think was that *Animal Care Specialist* would have been the perfect MOS for me . . . if I wanted to return to the farm after service.

A Friday in Airborne School was like a Friday anywhere else. We were all eager to rest our tired bodies and enjoy two days off. Two days with zero obligation to anyone but ourselves. We started our last day of ground week, uncanny enough, with another long run. A mass formation moving double-time but in slow motion. A paradox. Like watching Grandpa unload hay. "Hurry up, hurry up," he'd say, burning great energy at a fraction of my pace.

The first Black Hat leading our morning run could have sung professionally. His booming voice was warm and inviting as he called out lines like:

Airborne, airborne, all the way
Airborne, airborne, every day

Our spirits soared as we shuffled along, singing to this

pleasant beat. After a mile or so, Sergeant Airborne Palmer took charge of the formation and introduced a new cadence. The impending weekend must have left him spunky, as he sang:

Left-right, left-right, left-right, kill
Left-right, left-right, you know I will!

Some of us were apprehensive about this new song. Others—myself included—belted it out gleefully.

Our pace quickening, Palmer continued:

Runnin' through the campground
Where all the terrorists train
I pulled out my machine gun
And blood began to rain!

Commotion struck the rear of the formation and a new Black Hat sprinted up to Palmer. I was close enough to overhear something about the company commander. Palmer rolled his eyes and fell in with the rest of us. This new Black Hat began singing:

C-130 rolling down the strip
Airborne Ranger gonna take a little trip

After PT, I stumbled upon Sergeant Airborne Palmer getting chewed out by the company commander behind the DFAC.

"I don't want to hear those cadences again," Captain Raymond was saying. He had the look of a politician who had failed at being a movie star. Well-put-together but not photogenic enough to stand out in a crowd. His uniform badges were new and still retained their luster. Uniform badges I craved. Air Assault, Airborne obviously, but no combat patch on his right sleeve, unlike Palmer who swapped out combat patches per his mood, signaling he had deployed multiple times and with different units.

"Soldiers of all backgrounds come to Jump School," Raymond continued. "Some of us don't want to sing about knifing old ladies or stomping little birds."

Palmer took his admonishment stoically. But when Captain Raymond was out of sight, he let loose a shot-glass worth of brown spittle. It hit the pavement with a spidery splat. He turned and saw me, but I hurried away as if passing by.

Since day one, injured trainees were background props to any airborne setting. These poor souls could be seen crutching around the barracks or lingering at the DFAC over lukewarm coffee, a swollen ankle bandaged or braced or broken entirely in a cast of neutral colour; black or navy-blue, perhaps, but nothing bright and cheerful. They looked miserable. Defeated. They all had training stories, of course, if one dared to speak with them. Doing so felt like a séance, like reaching out to ghosts, their responses garbled and shy.

The most hopeful—the most vocal—were the potential recycles. Those who might recover from their sprains or strains fast enough to graduate with the class behind them. They were still a part of our community and could usually blame their injury on something reasonable, like the sudden emergence of ground during the night jump. Still, every pair of crutches I heard clicking on the sidewalk reinforced the idea that nothing was certain. There's a degree of chance to every military exercise. Even I, in all my enthusiasm, was not immune from a strong gust of wind affecting my landing, or the horrifying idea of someone floating below me, stealing my air, and momentarily collapsing my parachute.

Barnes wasn't as dismayed about becoming injured. Probably because his laptop held an impressive library of pirated movies and TV shows. In the event of an injury, he felt confident in his ability to twiddle away his convalescence watching season after season of *King of the Hill* or *The Wire*. I splurged on a tax-free laptop at the Post Exchange, and he shared his collection. We soon discovered an underground trading network of bootlegged media, tech-savvy privates holed up in the barracks swapping films as if exchanging phone numbers. And just like that, we had enough pixelated and grainy entertainment to last us our entire careers.

Tower Week

During the second phase of Airborne School, the gravity of combat parachuting—no pun intended—was becoming clearer as we practiced on a zip-line they could have charged money for. Although there was little chance of injury, there were consequences to our performance, and even some of the most squared-away students managed to bungle the exit procedure, myself included. Simple motions we practiced ad nauseum during ground week suddenly became elusive given the added variable of height. Standing in the thirty-four-foot tower, wearing a harness simulating a T-10D parachute, all we had to do was state our name and roster number, leap out, count four one-thousands, grip and check our imaginary canopy, and perform a parachute landing fall after gliding to fine cut grass.

Simple, no?

Well, there's training for something and then there's actually doing it. This tower exercise blurred the lines between the two.

Students would leap out without stating their name. They would leap out and forget to count. Count but then freeze. Leap out while shouting their name, like Geronimo. Any possible way you can imagine messing up this order—I saw it. From good soldiers, too.

These missteps posed a delicate question: How well would we perform next week in a real Goddamn airplane twelve hundred feet in the air?

Doubts swirled within me when the sergeant airbornes casually recounted horror stories of bad landings, describing snapped fibulas and torn ligaments in graphic detail. Sergeant Airborne Palmer spoke with delight in his eyes about the backward knee he once encountered and the shard of bone protruding from one private's shin the year before, an injury he personally attended to, splinting the leg and helping EMTs load the screaming young man into an ambulance.

Worse was the prospect of getting caught in a tree. If your parachute gets caught and the branches break, odds are it won't reopen before landing. This could be a fifty-foot fall, depending on the tree. If you get stuck, and I mean *really stuck*, procedure for getting down is to pop your reserve chute at your stomach and shimmy its chords like Tarzan.

It was alarming how much my confidence had waned by the end of week two. Infantry was already such a high-risk occupation; I began to wonder why the Army still offered Airborne School, with so much potential for a career-ending injury. Combat parachuting is seldom used in the field of battle; the last historic jump being early on in Iraqi Freedom. It's more a time-honored tradition at this point, a throwback to the *Band of Brothers* glory days. My ego was granted a small boost when I received uncharacteristic praise from Sergeant Airborne Palmer. It was during my final tower jump, waddling like an Oompa Loompa with a mock rucksack pressed against my thighs, I performed all actions beautifully. My name and number recited with bass, as if projected by a stage mic. I then proceeded to clear the tower, count, check canopy—I even remembered to drop the rucksack before impact. Rolling over from my landing, I spat out grass and saw Palmer scribbling across his omniscient clipboard.

"Nice job, Airborne," he said monotone, not looking at me. "Do that five times next week and you'll be okay."

This was considered high praise from him.

For some reason, even after nailing the final tower exercise, I couldn't shake the feeling that between now and graduation something would go horribly wrong.

Jump Week

You know those transitory hurry-up-and-wait moments I spoke of? Well, I discovered something worse. While it's misery to wait around idle when you expect something to happen, it's terror when you know something will happen.

Like the ascent and flight to the drop zone during my first live jump. We were seated single file, a line of green-gray uniforms donning parachutes like backpacks— edamame beans about to be ejected from their pod. Most faces had a stretched, hollow overlayer. A shine to their cheekbones, right below deep-set eyes. Some bit their nails or swallowed compulsively. Even Barnes—who was always so unperturbed—looked noticeably altered, clenching his jaw while taking deep inhales.

The Jump Master at the doorway shouted—and we echoed back: *Three minutes.*

Those three minutes became one minute, and we were told to stand up and hook our static lines to the cable above us. Checking the chute of the person ahead of us, we indicated their equipment was sound with a crisp slap to the ass. "Okay!" we shouted to this person, one by one, slap by slap, a quick game of physical telephone all the way to the Jump Master. I didn't know what to look for but figured any defect to the person's parachute would have been obvious.

It felt like my whole life was prologue to this defining moment. I'd spent eighteen years gestating and was about to be birthed out of a military aircraft.

A few more perfunctory checks were performed at the now open doorway, and I heard *Green light, go*, such a simple and intrinsic command, and the line emptied with the urgency of shoppers on Black Friday.

My body moved without consent from my faltering mind. I doubt it looked as sexy as I imagined. Closer and closer I edged toward the door, all but pushed by the person behind me, emboldened by the brave person ahead of me. I handed my yellow static line to the Jump Master and turned to face a rectangle of blue sky.

It's best not to think during moments like this. It's better to react and hope your training carries you through.

After not so much a jump as a step, my arced body was enveloped by hot air. There was a fractional moment where I was suspended freely before I felt a tug at my armpits, like being lifted as a toddler, lifted by the hands of God. Daring to open my eyes, parachutes looked like sentient jellyfish of the sky, bobbing and shifting around me. Warm bliss poured into me like hot wax conforming to mold. I'd never felt closer to life, toying with death in this way. A serene calm laced the panorama; it was as if we were training to descend with gifts of peace and love, not rifles and hand grenades.

A voice projected by bullhorn advised me to "Check canopy—check canopy. Gain canopy control." Then came the landing—my pillowy first landing. The softness of the grass. The joy in tumbling after my feet gently kissed the earth, like rolling down a sunny knoll on Easter morning.

I was smitten with this life. I was Infantry. And while I hadn't earned my Jump Wings yet, I felt like a true paratrooper.

After landing, it's mandatory to run toward the designated rally point to prove an injury was not sustained. That first run was a weightless, frolicking jaunt. We were calendar puppies bounding through a field of dandelions. Barnes belted a deep, uninhibited laugh as I raced up to him. We embraced, all but jumping up and down. Even though we had just shared the same experience, we found it necessary to recount each moment like kids discussing action scenes in a superhero movie.

> *"And then I jumped out and I was like—I'm flying!"*
> *"But her parachute bumped into mine, and we both slipped away."*
> *"I tried to keep my eyes on the horizon, but I couldn't help looking down."*
> *"After landing my chute started to drag—I was pulled like ten feet!"*

Exuberant stories like this were the sing-along songs on our bus ride back to Benning. At that moment, rank really did dissolve. Captains bumped knuckles with PFCs, while Sergeants and LTs beamed at one another. We all reveled in our mutual ability to jump out of a perfectly good airplane and land without dying.

Back at HQ, rumors were circulating that two privates had refused to jump. Chickened out. I knew it was true when I spotted the soldiers in question barely eating at the DFAC. They sat together and had a morphed physiology I had seen before. The same blank eyes and withdrawn demeanor of Infantry recruits who washed out of Sand Hill. I wondered if they should be put on suicide watch; their failure to prove their abilities was clearly a great burden, especially surrounded by so much jubilance they were now divided from. It was a small blessing there were two because at least they had each other. We made fun of the recruits who couldn't hack it during basic training, but no one dared comment on these two. Probably because we had all felt the same visceral fear that had gripped them. It was easy to imagine that fear getting the better of us, halting us in place, turning our bodies rigid at the doorway.

I realized then why the airborne tradition matters. Like the Army, Airborne School is voluntary. No one forces you to do this. Its stresses, both physical and psychological, reveal how a person might perform under duress. A soldier can have all the training in the world, but you'll never know how a person will react to a true life-or-death situation until they're in one. Jumping out of that damn airplane felt more real, more daunting than even the most elaborate field exercises, even the ones with special effects: controlled explosions and simulation rounds leaving bruises and red welts.

Having survived my first jump, I thought the proceeding four would be less taxing. But each time that C-130 took us skyward, the same fizzy unease corroded my insides.

I felt the most paranoia about the night jump. It was supposed to be our last one before graduation, but it became number four to accommodate an inclement forecast. When I exited the bird into pitch nothingness and felt the pull of my canopy opening, I had to trust by rate of descent that all was well. The lights flashing below gave us something to aim for. It was strangely hypnotizing, the exhilaration from previous jumps reduced to an uncertain trickle. My mind emptied its thoughts as I fell through a peaceful void, an interdimensional chasm existing alongside space and time. Then light from below flashed in my eyes, and I came to a sudden halt. I hit the ground hard and unprepared. The pain I felt was not nearly as terrifying as the sickening crunch I heard. Attempting to stand, my left ankle throbbed and refused to bear weight.

Because it was so dark, the Black Hats failed to notice me hobbling—practically crawling—from the drop zone to the bus. When we got to the barracks Barnes offered his shoulder and we ascended the stairs to our bunks. It was a sharp pain, removing my boot, which now felt two sizes too small.

"How does it look?" I asked Barnes, peeling off a stinky green sock. "Do you think it's broken?"

"How should I know?"

"You're a medic."

"A pet medic."

He poked where my ankle bone once was, and I winced, sucking in air through my teeth.

"Our final jump is tomorrow morning," he said.

It was all the pep talk I needed. Like an 80s montage, we set to work experimenting with several pain-mitigation plans. We fashioned a cardboard splint that fit snugly inside my thicker winter boots, and if I wore three pairs of socks and wrapped extra laces around the outside, I could at least stand and walk if I favored my right leg. True ingenuity comes from little means shaken with equal parts desperation.

Barnes went out and somehow procured an icepack at 2230 hours. He returned and passed it to me, saying, "You better pray we don't start tomorrow with a run."

It was impossible not to imagine being caught and recycled. I pictured myself lounging in airborne limbo, watching hour after hour of pirated TV while an undetermined fate hung above my head like The Paperwork of Damocles: sudden orders kicking me out of Airborne School and sending me back to my unit without Jump Wings, my ankle recoverable but my pride crushed forever.

The next morning I woke drenched in sweat. Immediately I thought it to be a fever from a broken ankle, then I noticed Barnes was sweating, too. We were all sweating. My ankle, while slightly less swollen, was no better or worse. Overnight the weather had turned tropical. So hot and humid, it was category five on the heat index. Category five meant extra hydration. Cat five meant *no running*. A fucking Christmas miracle in late July.

"You lucky SOB," Barnes said, laughing.

I'm no meteorologist, though it seemed the weather was cooking up a nasty southern storm. And with present skies clear, we piled in the bus for one last jump.

The added thirty-one pounds of the parachute were not kind to my ankle injury. Sergeant Airborne Palmer stood guard as we loaded the aircraft. He yanked me out of line:

"Winter boots," he said. "In this heat?"

The C-130's turboprop engines blew hot air like industrial hair dryers.

Studying the cardboard wedged around my heel and the extra laces wrapped around my boots, Palmer said, "What the hell kind of white trash CLS is this? Are you hurt?"

And as if he'd spoken a magic incantation summoning him, Captain Raymond appeared at his side. "Problem with this one, Sergeant?"

This was it. The moment I dreaded. I was so close. So close to feeling those wings stab my skin.

Palmer studied me, his coal-coloured eyes narrowed to a searching look, no doubt contemplating my fate.

"No, Sir," Palmer finally said. "Just thought this private's boots were untied." He turned to me: "You better hustle up, Airborne."

I walked as straight as I could, swallowing the pain. During the roughly one-minute descent after my canopy opened, I remember thinking that even if I break my ankle clean—I'd made it. I was a true paratrooper.

Maybe it was the adrenaline, nature's cure-all, but after completing that final jump, my ankle felt a tad more stable. With pride, slight discomfort, and the satisfaction of completing something lofty, I staggered off that drop zone and joined my brothers and sisters at the bus who were basking in the high of true accomplishment. Nothing could faze us.

Until the bus dropped us at HQ, right at the feet of Captain Raymond. He had called an impromptu formation to address a growing crisis. Arms akimbo, he walked our ranks dour-faced, the clouds above him equally menacing.

"Tomorrow you're all going to graduate Jump School," he said, and it would have been appropriate to shout for joy were it not for his pissy attitude.

"But tomorrow—you will *not* be getting blood wings."

I blushed. A spotlight had snapped on, singling me out in the crowd. He went on to explain, "for those who don't know," what blood wings were and the pressure the Army was under to eliminate such senseless hazing acts.

"Blood-pinning is juvenile and demeaning. Any sergeant airborne under my command caught performing such a ritual will face the strictest disciplinary measures I possess."

Fat drops of rain started pelting us. No one moved. We all watched Raymond with the same mistrust. How determined was he to assert his rank and education over us? Would he keep us out here to get soaked? But seconds later when he dismissed our formation, I wished he had kept us out, just to have had even greater reason to resent him.

That whole evening as the storm lashed our barracks, I stared out the window and stewed on his words. What kind of military was this? Literally months from now, some of us would be in Iraq or Afghanistan contending with live rounds and IEDs—and here we were Stateside being lectured about the sharp dangers of uniform badges? Between Captain Raymond and the shitty weather, my enthusiasm was gone.

I stood in formation that sunny graduation morning defeated, ready to move on. *Give me my token tinsel, I don't even care anymore.* I thought of all the paratroopers before me who had received blood wings and felt excluded from their ranks. As if they were somehow more airborne than me. I had endured so much to get here, and now graduation was just a perfunctory hurdle. Without the possibility of pain and blood creating a mnemonic marker of this moment, it all felt hollow and unnecessary.

The sergeant airbornes walked line by line, quietly affixing our new badges to our uniforms. Those who had family present could opt for their loved ones to do this instead. Barnes' uncle—the guy who talked him out of Infantry—chuckled toothily as he took the place of the sergeant airborne and aligned the jump wings above his nametape. He'd flown in for this honor. Columbus, Ohio to Columbus, Georgia.

I watched in a fit of jealousy as his uncle gripped the nape of his neck and with a meaty thumb pressed the badge into his chest. Pressed hard. A couple of soft punches to really drive it home.

No.

Barnes grimaced out a smile, and they laughed and hugged one another. Captain Raymond watched this happen; he had no authority over a civilian.

Barnes, you son of a bitch. *Do me—do me*! I wanted to cry but held my strict military bearing. The pet technician got blood wings from his uncle, and here I was, an Infantry paratrooper, being baby-sat by Captain Rulebook.

Sergeant Airborne Palmer came to pin my wings, which was an honor in its own right. He moved slowly, with the sad, uncertain eyes of a leashed animal.

"I know you wanted blood wings," he said. "Well done. You've earned these." The metal badge rested in his open palm and he sighed.

And then I saw it. It was magnificent. The bouncing, shining mustache of Drill Sergeant Shrader making its way through the formation. Civilian onlookers briefly touched their vacant upper lips in envy of his endowment.

"I'll take over from here," Shrader said with the voice of Superman. Palmer's extinguished eyes relit, as did mine.

Shrader was out of uniform and dressed in the Army's classic civilian attire: sensible tennis shoes, jeans, and a business-casual polo.

In an instant Captain Raymond was upon us. "Wait, Private, who is this man to you?"

Keeping my eyes forward—toward the horizon, I said: "He's my brother, Sir," which was true enough in the way that all Infantry servicemembers are indelibly united by the bond of combat, even if I'd yet to see any.

Shrader being "family," Raymond's rank held little weight.

"You didn't think I'd leave one of my privates hanging?" said Shrader. This sounded so much like one of the genius double-entendres he was famous for, I laughed heartily. I could kiss this ugly grunt who put me through so much pain and misery only a few weeks prior.

And when those cold points pierced my uniform and drove into my flesh, warm blood oozed out, staining my undershirt. The sight of it made me giddy. There was nowhere else I would have rather been. No other life I would have rather been living.

It was the most deserved thing I ever earned. And Grandma and Grandpa, I decided, would never hear a word of it.

On a Mountain in Logar

I.

NOTHING WAS THE SAME after we took incoming on OP Tiger Eye.

It was just before lunchtime. I was up on that mountain burning shit in a barrel when the mortars began to land. Before impact, I thought I'd heard the hollow "pop" of distant artillery, but hunched over, stirring a molten stew of human fecal matter, I placed little value in my senses. My eyes burned; I didn't dare open my mouth. Breaths were taken in short, controlled bursts, craning my neck sideways like a long-distance swimmer.

Sergeant Holloway stood about twenty meters back, supervising. Even at that distance he wore disposable blue gloves, just in case he might have to touch something associated with this task.

"It needs more gas—more gas!" he called to me as I worked the charred two-by-four clockwise. "Oh for the love of—" He threw his hands in the air and began striding toward me with the look of a disappointed father about to ignite a charcoal grill for a bumbling son.

This was when the first round struck and our deployment changed forever, but perhaps I'm getting ahead of myself . . .

Our cyclical two weeks up on OP Tiger Eye always felt like a mini vacation from the massive corporatey FOB we were posted at. If FOB life was an extended glamping trip: with showers, internet, and even fast food, then OP Tiger Eye was like roughin' it backcountry. We bathed ourselves with baby wipes, we ate strictly MREs, and our entertainment was our comradery, which often took the form of a lamp-fire ghost or girl story, fabricated or fact. We couldn't build a real fire at night for fear of outing our position, so a dim red headlamp was placed between us in lieu of real warmth. When this, too, was eventually deemed a risk, we told our stories in the dark.

By far the best storyteller was Specialist Grayson, who had some college under his belt in Film Studies. We enjoyed listening to him, but we couldn't trust his authenticity. It always felt like he was testing out Film-Studies craft on us, constantly deviating from the truth for the sake of spinning a more compelling yarn. The best lies are always an elaboration on simple truths.

Staff Sergeant Holloway was the more sincere storyteller, not to be confused with *the better*. This guy also understood the art of story. He had joined the Army just before 9/11, back when the military was preparing for Russian hordes, not insurgents hidden amongst shepherds. These two bards would often go tit-for-tat like a rap battle—first something youthful, vicarious, and larger than life and then something earnest and pertinent to our deployment.

One story that left a permanent bruise on my super-soldier ego was Sergeant Holloway's "Grenade" story. This story terrified me for its honesty. It made me confront emotions I was doing well at the time to avoid.

By mnemonic proximity, I also remember the tale

Grayson told that night, it wasn't his best, but much like Holloway's "Grenade" story, it might have been his most honest. Grayson's story also impacted me, impacted everyone, although its effects wouldn't be felt until much later in our deployment.

Newly twenty-one Grayson was rolling down I-5 at 0200 after partying at a cowgirl-themed club in downtown Sacramento. He was annoyed because he was stone-cold sober, transporting a Honda Civic-load of drunken college kids. One plucky tagalong in the back, affectionately referred to as Rumble-belly because of his husky physique, with no warning, with no request to pullover, rolls down the window and spews a stream of vomit. At sixty miles per hour, it was like unfurling a liquid banner of pink ribbons. The side of Grayson's car was painted by it. Rumble-belly, the poor sap, had been duped by the scantily clad cowgirls into consuming copious amounts of strawberry-flavored tequila. Ten bucks a shot, but they all "wooed!" while he tossed them back. To his credit, this poor kid, with his empty wallet and his empty stomach, was more than apologetic. "I promish I'm gonna cleen it for you, man. I'mma sooo sorrry."

This placated Grayson, and they all shared a good laugh at Rumble-belly's expense. Then the blue lights popped in his rearview mirror. They all thought they were instantly fucked in the way everyone panics and assumes guilt when confronted by authority. But taking inventory, they realized they had done nothing wrong: everyone was twenty-one, Grayson hadn't touched a drop, they had no booze in the car, he was going the speed limit.

That's when he noticed the trooper's wipers ticking left-right in double-time, fanning streaks of pink. The trooper's head was out the window as he came to a stop, that's how smothered his windshield was. He stormed up in that trooper/drill-sergeant hat and probably did some shit that was illegal. Grayson and

Rumble-belly were man-handled, and everyone was made to stand against the guard rail. The car was tossed: glove box, center console, trunk. Try as he might, there was nothing to arrest them on. Grayson blew a 0.0%; no one had any warrants. The more the trooper investigated the more volatile he became. Finally, Rumble-belly, in classic obsequious form, broke down and offered to clean the trooper's windshield. But with what? His shirt! His favorite Abercrombie shirt he bought because he thought it might improve his odds with the ladies, striped in blue and white. He pulled it off and his pointy, corpulent man-breasts swayed as he mopped up his own vomit. The trooper didn't exactly tell him to do this, but he didn't stop him either. When it was done, and they were released, Rumble-belly sat quietly in the back, bare-chested with his precious shirt stinky and balled up on his lap.

"So let that be a lesson to you, gents," Grayson said after finishing the story. "Always do the right thing. Even when you're doing the wrong thing."

As a combat arms unit, we had our fair share of DUIs, of bar fights, of run-ins with the law. Extrapolation on this phenomenon could be its own social study. Grayson's story almost had a cautionary edge to it. Something that might be told during a safety briefing. *Okay, you numbskulls—don't beat your wives, take it easy on the dog, but above all—do not, I repeat, do not—drink and drive . . . Now enjoy your three-day weekend.*

But then Grayson said something that changed not only the dynamic of his story but how we viewed him.

"But I must confess I haven't been entirely truthful," he said to us all. "For I told you I was the cool, confident driver bearing witness to quiet little Rumble-belly's humiliation. In fact—it was the reverse. Yes, my friends, fat little Rumble-belly was *me*."

Holy fuck. This was inconceivable. *Grayson used to be fat and awkward?* Why was this so tantalizing? I couldn't picture it. He wasn't a swole PT stud like Sergeant Holloway, but he was more than competent hiking around the steep terrain. He had an easy smile, surfer dude vibes, and was a go-to lower enlisted leader, despite not having much time in service.

"You're lying," someone just as perplexed as I called him out.

"No, it's the God's honest truth!" said Grayson, right hand raised.

We all thought the same thing: this reversal was a narrative twist, maybe something he snuck in last minute. Stories like this always hit harder in the first person. Grayson was just testing out new material. A bait-and-switch. We thought we were listening to a story on morals but really it was a story of an underdog, which Grayson clearly was not. Plus, we had all heard this story a thousand times before. The track and field coach who had knock-knee. Rocky Balboa. Arnold Schwarzenegger. Grayson's story was too archetypical. It would have been believable if injected in casual conversation: "My waistline used to be forty-two but look at me now in these Army greens!"

Passed off as a narrative, no one believed the college-educated and highly capable Grayson had once been shy and awkward, but we enjoyed his creative storytelling all the same.

II.

I should probably articulate the confusing origins of OP Tiger Eye. Much like Grayson's story, this too is going to sound like exaggerated reality, a picture-perfect fairytale: too coincidental to be true. But I assure you, to the best of my recollection—this is ninety percent real.

During pre-deployment planning, our unit believed OP Tiger Eye was named for its perfect oval shape on a topographic map, with the dozens of squiggly lines radiating from its peak resembling tiger stripes but also clueing us in as to how much a pain in the butt it would be to summit it, literally and figuratively. Let's just say you needed the eye of the tiger to conquer this beast. But would you believe an actual feline resided with us on the mountain? If that surprises you, imagine our surprise when we first occupy the area and discover a cuddly orange tabby living with the soldiers.

We had just hiked up for the first time—and already I wanted it to be the last time.

"Gentlemen, welcome to OP Tiger Eye," a staff sergeant from our counterpart unit said in a cheerful, peppy voice. He was going home; we were just arriving.

We pretty much collapsed at his feet. With our rifles, our rucksacks, our Kevlars and plate carriers, hiking up to OP Tiger Eye was no joke. We had trained for this, but it still broke us off like a stale KitKat bar. Anytime you see some high-speed, twenty-year-old ROTC kid on the Stairmaster in the gym wearing combat boots and plate carriers, he's training for the same thing. All I can say is Godspeed there, fella.

So, we were taking a tour of this mountain, drenched in sweat, our bodies so starved of sodium that warm water from our Camelbacks tasted like Mountain Dew, and this happy red cat emerged from a supply shack and rubbed against the staff sergeant's calves. We all thought we were hallucinating. It was unreal. An obvious glitch. Something from one world spliced into another. Like seeing a Goombah from *Super Mario Bros* waddle across a *Sonic the Hedgehog* game. This just shouldn't be. But it did. It did be.

"No one knows how he ended up on the OP," this sergeant explained to us. A couple of his joes had it in mind to name him Jack Bauer. Not after the show 24, but apparently after a legendary episode of *It's Always Sunny in Philadelphia* where the gang adopts a junkyard tomcat and gives him this name. His soldiers ran around for about a day calling the cat *Agent Jack Bauer* before they realized that the words *Home of Chester* were spray-painted in redrum font on the back of the supply shack. After a few rounds of back-and-forth deliberation, taking into consideration that he responded to *Chester*, they went with this name. And so did we.

He was beautiful, with murky green eyes, flaring ear tufts, and distinctive stripes intimating a bit of wild left in him from his distant ancestors. Very fitting, for this petite and playful kitty, who in another life could have lived a plush existence as lap cat to my mom, was a ruthless killer. Every other day we would find a new bird carcass deposited somewhere on the OP. But despite his murderous proclivity, he was a loving little critter who warmed our souls by the very brightness of his fur.

Living outdoors in such primitive conditions, our minds naturally grew more spiritual. I'd often find myself stargazing at night, imagining a genesis for OP Tiger Eye. Before we came with our airlifted Connex container acting as a barracks, before we marched up with our optics and sandbags and belts of grenades for the MK 19, before all this there was only a mountain and a cat. We were here now—as guests—but before us there was only Chester. It was clear that this mountain belonged to him.

III.

Doing my absolute best to remain true to his likeness, Sergeant Holloway's "Grenade" story went something like this:

I did Iraq in '03. Now that was a war. Shock and awe, baby. None of this pussyfootin' around counterinsurgency BS. It was glorious to see the full might of the U.S. Military unleashed. Glorious but also terrifying to live under the constant threat of mayhem. Everything felt precise and coordinated yet also unexpected. "Christ!" I remember thinking after seeing a 1,000-pound JDAM go off: "I didn't think it would be that bright." You always have an expectation of how something's going to be, and then you have reality, but there's also this chaotic middle ground. That's where I existed when they first handed out grenades.

Our supply guy brought them out in bulk with a clipboard, just like any other piece of issued equipment. We even had to sign for them back then. I was like: "So if I pop this sucker and have nothing to clear supply with—what then? Will I owe the Army money?" My squad leader told me not to overthink it.

"Just have it on your person and pray you never have to use it," he said.

They gave us the same little pouches we have now to secure it to our flak jackets. Only the flak jackets of yesteryear aren't nearly as high-speed as the IOTVs today. I couldn't place that grenade nowhere without it being a bother. Down low worked well until you dropped in the prone to shoot, then you had this apple-sized bomb digging into your appendix. I eventually settled on having it up high near my heart, where it was in constant view of my periphery. It was like having a second nose, it was always in sight, unavoidable no matter where my head turned. But unlike my nose: I couldn't seem to ignore it long enough to forget that I had it. It became this fraught alien appendage, something I grew increasingly worried about as the war progressed.

Now, a grenade, like a bayonet, is almost an antiquated item. You can't throw a grenade very far. At best, you'd chuck it in a bunker—or more likely someone's living room—and hope it does the hard part for you. This was probably what my squad leader meant by saying "pray you never have to use it." If you whip out a grenade in a firefight, that is some desperate close-quarter shit you got yourself into. None of this was lost on me as I carted my grenade around from block to block, city to city; its sheer weighty hang reminding me that at any given second—something had the potential to blow up in my face.

Maybe I'd have been more confident had I received the proper training. But to this day it's a dirty secret that I never qualified with grenades. Yes, you heard that right. I swam through the course, just like all y'all, no doubt. Then it came to the live-throw, and I was ejected from the pit after my first toss. See, one of the drill sergeants had placed his green, big-ass hat on the middle mannequin, and all the troops wanted to stick their grenade closest to that target. When I threw mine, instead of ducking behind the protective wall, I watched open-mouthed as my grenade landed in the patch of shade made by the drill sergeant's hat. Maybe I wanted to watch that stupid hat blow up, maybe I was stunned at such a lucky toss. I must have stared a little too long, 'cause I found myself slammed against the wall by the supervising cadre who pressed over me like he was saving my life. I didn't get to throw my other two grenades to qualify. I thought I was a no-go, a failure. Well, they must have needed fucking soldiers—and stat—'cause I was pushed through to graduation without a word about it. They couldn't afford to reject or recycle anybody after 9/11.

Here's the funny, true part: the drill sergeant's hat was no worse for the wear. Literally. He dusted it off and stuck it back on his fat, bald head right after I'd blown it skyward and six feet back. It made me think: "What good are these things? Other than making such an awful racket."

So, is there such a big difference between throwing one grenade and three? Well, it took Goldilocks three tries to find the right porridge, the right bed. I was strapped with something on my chest too hot and too hard for me to be comfortable with. My heart literally beating against it. We were seeing some real shit, too. On some occasions, enemy bullets were close enough to communicate their "crack" or their "bizz" or their "thump" or their "sizzle." We were quickly becoming fluent in the many dialects of death, yet I couldn't shake the anxiety of my own grenade. I just knew the day would come when I'd get shot in the grenade, or I'd roll over on it wrong, or intense desert sunlight would superheat it and blow my head off, cartoonishly intact and pouting like the remains of a suicide bomber.

Then one day on patrol, we take contact. By the time we find cover we realize it's coming from above. So, we start lighting up this rooftop-alcove thingy, but we're at the wrong angle, chipping at a wall while the insurgent points his AK down and fires blind. My squad leader shouts for me to arc a grenade while everyone else suppresses fire.

Let me just pause and say to all y'all privates: this is a bad idea. Usually you throw "from" the rooftop, that way you're not fighting gravity. But whatever, pinned down, being shot at, being yelled at, I take my stupid grenade—pull pin—and hurl it. It doesn't make it. It clips the lip of the rooftop, bounces back and lands right between my feet. I freeze, dumbfounded. I almost feel like laughing. I knew this fucking grenade would kill me. That's when I get tackled from behind. Basic training all over again, only this time it was one of the most selfless acts I've ever witnessed. My squad leader smothers me. We stay like this cringing and flexing and gnashing our teeth for five seconds . . . ten seconds . . . and nothing. The grenade was a dud. After we call in an airstrike for the shooter on the rooftop, we learn to never speak of this moment again.

My squad leader's risky decision to have me throw a grenade "up" was negated by the sacrifice everyone saw him make. People considered putting him up for an award, but then we'd have to document the whole debacle in greater detail. Back at

Saddam's palace, I kick my feet up and realize this whole time I was afraid of nothing more than a paperweight. Admittedly, it felt good to be rid of it. To have this empty camo pouch that once housed such paranoia. That's when the supply guy comes around, having heard about our exploits, he issues me a shiny new grenade. And yes, I have to sign for it. This time, though, I'm not quite so worried. I'd thrown two. If the first one was too hard and hot, and the second one too soft and cold, I figured if I had to pop this new grenade, it would have turned out juuust right.

But he never threw a third grenade. Not because he was afraid, but because the occasion never arose. "I'm the sergeant, but all of you privates have still thrown more grenades than me," he openly admitted. Even though that was true, he *had* thrown a grenade in combat. We all looked at our own grenades a little differently after his story. Especially me as the squad's grenadier. I carried not only a hand grenade but a bandoleer of 40mm rounds around my waist like a cop belt. A walking, talking, gum-chewing IED. But not an Improvised Explosive Device, an *intended* explosive device. Sergeant Holloway's stark honesty differed from the usual tune the Army was whistling at that time. Advice we were either told explicitly or arrived at ourselves.

Even if I wanted to be concerned about the ordinance I wore, I know what most leadership would have said: "Don't think about it, Private. Pretend you're invincible. You're Captain Fucking America, aren't you? You can't die. Not from your own grenade. What kind of a piss-poor story would that make?"

IV.

Whenever we cycled away from OP Tiger Eye and ran regular missions out of the FOB, I always felt an inner longing for that mountain and that cat. Features I was becoming increasingly possessive of, my mountain, my cat. I just couldn't wait for the next few weeks to end, until it would be our turn up there again. I thought about what it would take to rehome Chester to the FOB where we would be able to better care for him and he would have the opportunity to enliven so many other troops. This was impossible, however; his existence was already contested.

When First Sergeant found out a cat was up there with us, he commanded over the radio for us to "Get rid of it." The warming weather would make Chester a flea magnet. Plus, we didn't know what sorts of diseases he might already be carrying.

Sergeant Holloway looked at me, radio mic in hand, and put his career on the line for my cat. "I'm not sure that would be wise, Top. He's doing a good job keeping the mice out of the MREs."

"The mice. On a mountain?"

"Roger, Sergeant. The mountain mice. Yeah, they're up here."

Nothing to say of the effect Chester had on our morale, which wouldn't have contributed much to the conversation.

Brief static over the radio, before First Sergeant said, "Fine. Whatever. Just don't none of you get bit by him. If that happens, I'm hiking up there to kill him myself."

With First Sergeant's threat out in the open, I was never confident Chester would be there when we returned. I would sit at the FOB and worry some dumb private from second platoon would antagonize him—get bit—and that would be the end of it. Fortunately, I think my brothers relished this spunky kitty about as much as I did. In the end it would take something much worse to separate Chester from his mountain.

My mom was delighted to learn we had a cat in Afghanistan. So amused by this fact that the next care package she sent included more creature comforts for Chester than for me. This was how I earned my inevitable callsign. See, we would always open our mail Christmas style, really draw it out to make the most of it. This way we could also consider what trades to make. "One of my Copenhagens for one of your Marlboro reds? . . . Yo, can I get that copy of *Guns & Ammo* after you? . . . No way—Grayson got Gushers!"

On this particular occasion, I cut into my long-awaited care package greedily expecting a new game for my Nintendo DS and a month-long supply of jalapeno beef jerky. Instead, I found the latest issue of *Cat Fancy* magazine and a dozen cans of Fancy Feast. The same look of hysteria spread across everyone's face after flipping the cardboard flaps to reveal these commodities swimming in a bed of pink packing peanuts. By the time the laughter ceased, there wasn't a dry eye in the hooch.

At lights-out, when the whispers of conversation started snuffing out, Grayson called out in the dark, "Good night, Fancy Cat," and ignited another round of laughter. I laughed too, believing it to be a one-off. One final nightcap to an evening of jokes at my expense. When Sergeant Holloway greeted me the next morning with "Good to see ya, Fancy Cat!" I knew this was now my designator and there was nothing I could do about it. You don't choose your own callsign, anyone who tries is lame. *Can I be Arrow*? I remember one new guy asking. After Green Arrow, the comic book character. We called him Green Peen, instead.

So, my new name with all its derivatives was okay by me. I went to sleep that night an unknown PFC with the boring role-*based nomenclature of 1-7D, but I awoke reborn as* The FC. The Foxtrot Charlie. The dude who sacrifices his own junk food to feed a stray animal. The Fancy Cat.

Twelve cans of wet food equaled thirty-six ounces packed inside my rucksack, which felt like thirty-six *pounds* halfway up the mountain. Maybe it was delirium from exhaustion—my brain flooded with endorphins—but I was sure I'd attained some measure of enlightenment after suffering to lug all this up to Chester. He devoured the first tiny can of beef and poultry with gusto. Licked his chops after, unashamedly approving of American consumerism.

I was a needle-thin cog in a vast machination of war and order. But if I could do this one small thing—feed and care for this animal—then within my humble means I would have fostered goodness. But what if I could do more than that? What if I could get him back to the States somehow? You hear stories all the time of soldiers on deployment rescuing animals. Admittedly, this was selfish romanticism, as there had to be a local shelter or nonprofit in the country that would have taken him. Probably all the way in Kabul, but Kabul is a hell of a lot closer than Kansas. Although Kabul strangely seemed like the more unfeasible of the two. Imagine running that mission by the first sergeant? *Yes, I would like to use manpower, resources, instruments of war to escort a tabby a few hours north to the capitol of this rugged nation. Maybe we can make a PR thing out of it. Think of the book and movie options . . .*

But I never had the opportunity to rescue Chester. On the day in question, the first mortar landed nowhere near Holloway and me, but its impact was still scarier than anything I'd experienced thus far. We both ate dirt fast and stared at each other in the prone, the fear in our eyes burning like sparklers in cold December. A partly vicarious fear. See, the latrine was a decent hike outside of the OP, for obvious reasons, but the round struck dead-center of the compound. It would have been preferable for them to hit me and Holloway; then they'd at least have to walk their rounds to the real target. Somehow these fuckers scored a direct hit on their first guess. A direct hit on eight of my brothers. My sympathetic nervous system went on overdrive: stimulating nerve bundles around my solar plexus to shunt blood from my stomach to my legs that I might fling my weapon aside and sprint for the relative safety of the opposite direction. But this sensation was overpowered by an empathetic fear for the safety of others. A very different sort of dread housed in my throat and urging me not away from—but toward the danger.

We'd all experienced indirect fire at the FOB before, but that was almost passive compared to being on this dime-sized tip of mountain. If a round even found its way onto the FOB, there were bunkers, alarm systems, and vast open spaces where most ordinance would explode with menace but without harm. Teams stood by to provide counterfire, and the only responsibility for people like myself was to act like a seasoned Midwesterner staring down a tornado-green sky on their porch with a can of PBR—wait and inevitably the danger would pass.

On the OP, however, we were alone and limited in our response capabilities. Fortunately, Sergeant Holloway's first command after kicking into gear was to send me to higher ground, up the only jagged slice of mountain taller than the OP. "Get the fuck up there and see what you can see," he said. This felt like an acceptable middle ground to the conflicting flight-*no*-stay-and-fight phenomenon my body was grappling with. Holloway: the guy who openly admitted a phobia of spontaneous explosions bravely sprinted toward the OP. Now, you have to believe me when I say—I don't have the best recollection of what happened next. I wasn't in the midst of it, of any of it, really. But apparently, the boys at the OP didn't require my eagle eye to identify the origin. Holloway and a quiet, pasty-skinned PFC who wore forever tinted lenses and who no one expected very much of, together they slung hundreds of 40mm rounds Rambo-style from the Mk 19 until our resident mortarman could respond with artillery of his own.

The memories that are distinct are the images afterwards. Descending to the OP, smoke and little baby fires actively smoldering like the slopes of Mount Doom. And hearing Grayson cry out in agony.

"Aw fuck! I'm fucked—Jesus!"

He was on his ass, picking at his plate carrier and then tugging at his belt, trying to remove either, not realizing he couldn't do both at once. A medic rushed to him, sling bag spilling out supplies. I joined too, then another. We three pulled the safety lanyard and his IOTV fell apart like it was only ever male stripper wardrobe at a bachelorette party. We always thought this was a funny feature. Sometimes we yanked these lanyards as a prank, like flicking a dude in the balls. Then they had to stop and put their kit back together again. Pulling one on someone crying and rolling around in the dirt had a different feel to it.

The medic snipped his shirt with scissors so we could scan his midsection for blood. For shrapnel wounds, for intestines crowning out, for purple lumps or other such discolouration denoting a broken rib or a ruptured spleen. We parted the shirt halves, bracing for the worst, and gasped at what we saw.

Stretch marks. Bright and red, jagged and inflamed from the heat and pressure of his IOTV. The battle scars of rapid weight loss, which looked so much like real cuts the medic dabbed a roll of white gauze over them just to be sure.

"Grayson, where's it hurt, man?" the medic asked.

"All over," he cried.

We log rolled him, slid his pants halfway down his thighs.

"What about internal injuries?" I conjectured. If this was the case, it wasn't obvious.

Dirt and specks of gravel peppered his face and hands, but nothing life-threatening.

Shining a penlight in his eyes, the medic said, "He's fucked up, for sure. Yet somehow, by the grace of God—or just dumb fucking luck—there's no entry wounds."

"Grayson, where are we, man?"

"Soccer camp," he said in a sob.

The medic and I traded looks. Under different circumstances, we probably would have found that amusing.

"Can you sit up?" the medic asked. And when he did, on his own accord, we all started to breathe a little easier.

Grayson was medevac'd for good measure. A chopper came in, and he walked himself onto it, against his wishes. He kept telling us, "Guys, I'm fine. I'm fine, guys." A slight wobble to his g's. He did seem okay. But Lord knows that an hour later or next morning even, a line of blood might appear under his nose and he would drop dead in seizure. We couldn't take that risk. Holloway hugged him before he got on the bird. Kissed him on the forehead.

"You're gonna get a Purple Heart out of this, brother." He poked him in the ribs and joked about how it might help him Stateside with the ladies.

Sans Grayson, the mood at the OP was noticeably altered. We spent the remainder of the day quietly filling sandbags, cleaning our guns, doing what we could about our hygiene. Mentally preparing for the next attack. Would they hit us again? Yes. That was a certainty we needed to prepare for. We were so busy worrying about this fact, we failed to notice day turn to evening, evening to night. Suddenly it was twilight, and I remembered I had a cat to feed. This pleased me. I peeled open a can of Fancy Feast, tuna in gravy this time, and placed it outside the supply shack.

"Get it while it's good," I called to him.

He didn't show, so I got on all fours and started poking around. I remembered how my mom would summon our cats at nightfall. Tough-ass soldiers were brooding around the OP, eating chow and taking baby wipes to the ash on their faces, and here I was running around calling sing-song like: "Chester. Here kitty-kitty-kitty-kitty." But no one said shit about it. They all just watched me with looks of pity.

To this day, I've no idea what became of him. I like to believe that unlike us humans, Chester couldn't override his sympathetic nervous system to stand and fight with us. He was smart. He turned tail and ran for safety. Found it on some other mountain where bombs were not prone to fall from the sky. I really couldn't blame him for deserting us; we had brought something unholy to his mountain. Of course, some of the fellas had an alternative theory about what happened to him, but I prefer my version.

Holloway and the others were at the center of the OP, gazing out through optics, their heads on a swivel, a permanent state of alertness. Sound practice but also very taxing. The MK 19 was cleaned, greased, and ready to go again at the slightest stir of anything other than friendly forces.

"Hey bro," Holloway said to me as I approached.

"Sergeant," I replied, dutifully matching the sober energy around me.

This was usually the point in the evening when Grayson or Holloway would enrapture us with a story or two. I wanted to break the tension. Keep the tradition going. I thought about saying: "So I guess Grayson used to be fat, after all," but the spell was already broken. Grayson was en route to a hospital in Germany. Chester was gone. And no one wanted to hear any more stories.

JACK FLEMING LIVES!

OKAY—LET ME SET THE RECORD STRAIGHT. It started as a bunch of rumors first, before we lost control of it. But it really started as a stupid word game at a mission briefing.

"Your porn name!" LT began. "Pet's name and the street you grew up on."

He was keen on figuring out everyone's combination. Mine was Bella Tulane. Not bad if I was a chick. We got some other good ones: Snickers Calhoun, Georgie Wilder, Sherry Potts. Then this quiet, young private comes in and LT demands his info.

"Uh. Jack Fleming," the kid says, and our jaws drop.

There is a moment of silence before LT says, "My God, that's a handsome name," bringing fingertips to temples like it's too much for his brain to process.

"*Jaaack Flemmming*," Sergeant Kim tries it out, and sure enough, it's as smooth on the lips as it sounds in the ears. A phonetic Adonis.

Rivera starts slow clapping like this kid just did something Silver-Star worthy. It wasn't just Rivera; we were all possessed by the garish weight this name carried.

"Jack Fleming could be an American James Bond," I say.

"Very classy, indeed," LT agrees. "The type of name that'll wine and dine you—before taking you back to its apartment for a tender pounding."

This poor kid spoils our fun by telling us that Jack is a fluffy white Maltese, and Fleming is a residential byway in meth-town USA. We get a few more jokes out of it and then stop laughing when the captain comes in so we can all shout "at ease" at the top of our lungs. Captain throws a pen at Rivera, who's the loudest, and we're once again reminded that people will most likely try to kill us on our next mission passing out rice and beans.

We go about our business the next few days with no mention of Jack Fleming. Like any good improv joke, it was kind of a one-time deal. Outside of that briefing room it wouldn't have made much sense.

Then the Battle of Jowgi River happens. You might have heard of this one: Taliban down a Black Hawk and decide to ambush the rescue party. You haven't? Well, we get out there; it's outside our AO, but we're available so we go. These pararescue guys are dug in on the wrong side of the river. They had already recovered the pilot's remains and incinerated the bird, and they're taking heavy fire by the time we arrive, trying to decide if they should risk getting wet running or just fight their asses off. And Rivera—crazy sonofabitch—starts laying down 240, and he is just on-point, I mean—we're watching bodies drop while these PJs are stringing a rope across the river to exfil. I'm surprised Rivera didn't burn the barrel off—he was just rolling in brass by the end. So, the PJ guys get away, and they come up on our net flabbergasted.

"Who's the maverick on the 240?" they ask. "We want to know the name of the man who saved our lives."

Rivera is just all pink. I mean, we respect the hell out of these guys, shit—most of us wanna *be* these guys, or Rangers or SF or what have you.

"Aw, geez," Rivera says, twisting his foot like a schoolgirl. "Tell 'em . . . tell 'em Jack Fleming did it. Yeah, *Jack Fleming* is a machine-gun Mozart."

It made us laugh pretty good.

And that was just about the birth of it. We can blame it all on Rivera. If he wasn't such a humble prick . . . You see, he set the precedent. Anyone did anything cool afterwards— Jack Fleming got the credit.

—Jack Fleming shot and stopped a VBIED, though it was really Kim

—he CPR-revived a choking baby; LT did that one

—unearthed and snipped an IED

—rendered aid to an Afghan cop missing an arm

—befriended a pugnacious village elder

—attended Mosque with a terp and locals

—found multiple weapons caches

—got all our confirmed kills

The list goes on. Anything even remotely noteworthy, we all just said Jack Fleming did it. Why? Fuck, I don't know. We were bored, I guess. Even I caught two dudes at 0300 pushing an IED in a wheelbarrow and said Jack Fleming spotted them. Saw them clean and green through an LRAZ atop a cliffside OP. Called it in; got put in for a medal. Though back at the FOB and outside of official paperwork, me getting these guys was a rumor added to the growing list of miracles performed by one Jack Fleming. For some reason this felt more meaningful than another stupid ribbon for my Class A's.

Now I first started to suspect we had opened Pandora's gossip-box when my little cousin serving in Iraq's drawdown messages me on Facebook. My deployment had ended, and I was back in Fayetteville being pulled around the mall by my preggers wife Christmas shopping. So, I check my phone while she's checking juicers or salad spinners or some such nonsense, and there it is:

> Hey Cuz! You ever serve with a Jack Fleming? Might have been around during your rotation?

My first instinct—apart from laughing my ass off—is to push this farce as far as I can before coming clean with the truth.

> Fuck yes, I did! Jack Fleming is the goddamn patron saint of mayhem! You know how many lives he saved by being so deadly? No one wanted to do shit for ops without Jack Fleming covering our six!

Now, what he says next causes me to pause. Maybe I feel chills, too.

> Well, he's here in Iraq! Must have volunteered for another deployment. I haven't met him, but it gives me peace of mind knowing he's out there.

So, once we get home from x-mas shopping, I call up LT, Kim and Rivera and tell them we might have a little problem on our hands.

We figure it's highly improbable our collective imagination gave birth to some sort of phantom Fleming—if that's what you're thinking. More likely there's some poor bastard in Iraq who just so happens to be named Jack Fleming. Some unwitting private who we just turned into a wartime legend. You hear our rumors, then you pass a fit-looking kid at the FOB rockin' *Fleming* nametape, and you think: *could it be*?

We figure it's probably best just to let this one run its course. We've seen a few shenanigans in our time. For a hot minute, after this one episode of Family Guy, everyone was shouting *Roadhouse*! at anything requiring the least amount of physical effort. Well, we stopped saying roadhouse after so long, so we figure we'd all stop with the Jack Fleming bullshit, too.

But uh... Man, was I ever wrong on that account.

We get sent out to endure us some more freedom, this is over a year later, mind you. Different crew, but still got Rivera, Kim, and LT is now a captain.

We land in country eager to meet our ANA counterparts and quickly realize the whole Jack Fleming thing has spiraled out of control. Beyond your desert-variety war stories. I'm talking mythic proportions. You can't so much as take a shit without seeing graffiti about an impossible sniper shot made by Jack Fleming. You hear people in the chow hall chatting about the orphans he carried out of a fire or the high-risk livestock he helped birth. Stranger stuff than that, stuff people have no right believing in. How he shot an RPG out of the sky. That there's really three Jack Flemings, triplets who enlisted at the same time. One Jack Fleming donated a kidney to another Jack Fleming who got shot—I mean, it's just getting bizarre. Kim comes up and swears he saw a Jack Fleming morale patch worn by some Navy Seal types. Apparently, it's a cartoon face of a sly 1950s-era alpha male: Ray-Ban sunglasses, a dimpled chin and slicked-back hair. An acronym in gold underneath: *WWJFD*?

Even the ANA are hip to the Fleming mania. We'll be sitting before heading out on a patrol, and they're rattling off Pashto: "*Something, something, something*—Jack Fleming!—*something-something-something*," and they all start laughing.

The more this goes on, the more I rue the day we ever discovered the name.

It's worse for Rivera. While it annoys me, it terrifies him. Maybe it's his strong Catholic morals, prohibitions against lying and all that, or maybe he feels more responsibility because—as I said—he started all this.

"I'm freaking out, man," he says. "I can't eat. I can't sleep. I'm not worried about getting schwacked by the Taliban, I'm worried about what people are going to do when they find out we've been stealing our own fucking valor."

"Calm down," I say. "People don't actually believe in Jack Fleming in that way—it's just a gag."

"The other day I saw two local national kids huddled over a drawing book. I approached with a smile expecting to see Ninja Turtles or some shit, but—*no*—it's a custom-made Jack Fleming coloring book. Someone designed it and ordered up a plethora online. They're all over Afghanistan, man!"

"Okay," I say. "But what can we do? This is bigger than us now."

"We have to put Jack Fleming to bed."

"Yes, but how?"

"I don't know. But it has to be huge . . .

We look at each other and Rivera says:

"We're going to have to kill Jack Fleming."

So, we put on our murdering-hats and spend an inordinate amount of free time scheming how to pull it off. It sort of feels like trying to kill King Arthur. You can't just make up lore; these things unfold organically.

And then OP Tiger Eye gets overrun. Now, I know

you've heard of this one. It had been hit once or twice before, yet from what I gather it was a fairly chill place to kick back and survey the land. Well, the boys up there at the time get ejected, practically tumble down the mountain. A Taliban flag flies up the pole. Prudent thing to do would be to send out a drone, forget we were ever up there. Well, when QRF responds they light up the mountain with indiscriminate 50-cal, just as an f-you on their way out. This starts up a damn-near four-hour firefight neither side wants to break from. OP Tiger Eye is a landfill by the end of it. We take some casualties, and there's even an MIA who never made it off the mountain. *Real fog of war* shit. It's the perfect opportunity we need to kill Jack Fleming.

We spread the seeds of hearsay far at first, and it's amazing how quickly it doubles back to us. Any FOB we visit outside of our AO we circle up and gab about Jack Fleming's untimely demise. We write in Sharpie on DFAC tables:

Jack Fleming, KIA OP Tiger Eye.
God rest his beautiful soul

And you know what? It takes. Better than we could have hoped. A little too well. People go into public mourning. FOB Fleming gets erected. I'm seeing little candle-lit vigils outside of MWR hooches. It seems the only thing we did by killing Jack Fleming was cement his legacy. Looking back, I'm not sure why we expected a different outcome. Course, everyone present at OP Tiger Eye claims "It's not true. Jack Fleming wasn't even there. Which means . . . he's still alive!" This—I guess—is how a series of counter rumors gets started. Kim tells us that he heard from a Marine out in Helmond that his terp heard from a jingle truck driver that Jack Fleming secretly married a war widow and now lives peacefully with the local population out in Mazār-i-Sharīf.

Luckily, these marriage rumors are branded conspiracy and most go on believing Jack Fleming perished.

We edge closer to heading home and it becomes increasingly clear we must do the right thing and shatter the Jack Fleming mythos. People can't go on believing something that doesn't rightly exist. Also, Rivera will probably need psychological counseling. Not for PTSD, but he can't live with these lies any longer. They're corroding his insides.

A soft-spoken ANA sergeant approaches and asks if we know Jack Fleming's wife and children back in the States, and Rivera starts trembling like he's about to spontaneously combust.

"Please tell his family," this sergeant says to me, "that we are praying for God's peace to surround them during this sorrow."

"That's such a kind sentiment, Hakim. I'll make sure they know!"

And Rivera stares me down with the look a man makes right before he stabs you in the fucking face. I tell him it just wasn't the right time or person.

We decide the "right time" is conveniently our last day in country. Captain—formerly LT—holds an emergency formation, a "family meeting" as he calls it. The ANA form up, too, and Rivera, Kim and I march out, somewhat informally.

Kim starts us off. "We just wanted to say a few words about . . . Jack Fleming."

Heads lower in reverence.

Kim looks at me, looks at Rivera. No one wants to be the one to squeeze the trigger. Rivera stands in awe before this humble formation of both Afghan and American soldiers. Hard-working people, a little rough around the edges, who believe in a better world so much that they're willing to die for it.

"Fuck it," I say, using aggression to hype me up. "Listen here, men. You people need to know that Jack Fleming is nothing but a big, fat—"

"American hero!" Rivera practically pushes me over shouting this. He looks left, he looks right. "And Afghan hero," he says. "A hero to two nations. And I'm proud to have served with such a man. But he wasn't extraordinary. He was just like you and just like me. Having Jack Fleming on our side didn't give us a superhuman advantage out there. He was a simple man who only wanted to do his best. And his best was pretty damn good. He wanted to be good. As we all aspire to be. And I think you know that deep down we all have the capacity to be our own Jack Fleming."

The formation ends in mass applause. We're clapping, some are crying. As this goes on, Kim leans into Rivera and says, "So, I'm pumped and all, but what happens when we get back and the president wants to award nine posthumous Medals of Honor to Jack fucking Fleming?"

Rivera stares at the ground through twitching eyes.

"I'm getting the fuck out of the Army," he says.

LEARNING TO BE YOU

YOU GROW UP BELIEVING in your God-given destiny to (1) seek adventure, (2) slay the beauty, and (3) rescue the dragon. So, when the war presents itself as an opportunity to check-mark all three, finally your life begins. You've spent eighteen years evading trouble in an opioid-addled town, you've got a 2.2 GPA, but now your life is brimming with possibility. Your country has issued you a time-honored identity, allowed you to subsume a warrior archetype. You've dreamt of this moment since middle school. It's as if your temperament is finally able to express itself through meaningful action. The dormant cells of your body awaken! For years you've been testing combinations on the Da Vinci-Code cryptex housing your soul: *Fitness Trainer, Construction Worker, Student*; turns out it was *Soldier* all along.

Before you can become this perfect ideal, this ultimate version of yourself, first they must unmake you. Shout and scream and tear into you. Rip away all those pesky aspects of your personality which are not conducive to their grand designs. Luckily, their goals and your goals align, and you rise like a phoenix from basic training, earning accolades along the way. You relish the suffering but secretly question what it all adds up to: you barely qualified at shooting, your fitness is worse than when you arrived, and the week-long hospitalization for pneumonia nearly had you recycled to week 1. Mainly the training gave you the ability to eat shit and smile. Not to question your role in the scheme of things. To let others—who haven't the slightest clue what it means to be you—make decisions on your behalf.

Special Forces, you're told, are inundated from such tyranny, so the idea of joining their elite ranks spreads through your psyche like fungi; soon enough, you're possessed by the hope of ascending to an even narrower hierarchy. One day, you say, you'll get your chance. Until then your contract lists you as *11-Bravo*, plain old blister-footed Infantry. Part of the 20%, not the 2%. Fall in line and obey the same type of petty orders that kept the Old Testament tribes alive.

> — *You! Drink water . . .*
> — *Do pushups . . .*
> — *Stop picking that scab . . .*
> — *Cut your hair . . .*
> — *Stay away from junk food . . .*
> — *Don't piss off your battle-buddies . . . and wash your hands, goddamn it.*

In March, you were sworn in and by October you're already in Afghanistan. They tell you being an MRAP driver for the platoon sergeant is an important task. So important, learning to operate the fourteen-ton dump truck takes half an hour. A pot-bellied plainclothes contractor shows you how the tan behemoth works. He probably makes more in a year than you'll make your entire enlistment. You do as he instructs. The cargo ramp activates with the flip of a switch. He offers high praise for your ability to weave between traffic cones.

"Try backing it up ass-left. Okay, ass-right. Good. You're ready for war."

Welcome to war. Here kids swarm you on patrol, asking

for simple things like pens and candy. Despite the obvious tension carried by each local, it's easy to see a culture of warmth and hospitality exists in your Area of Operations, coming from many individuals who seem sadly uneducated and vastly ill-informed. One villager confuses your platoon for the Soviet Army that invaded the country in the 1980s, and nothing your interpreter says convinces him otherwise. *Another empire is trying this*, you imagine this man thinking. *Preposterous.*

There is constant talk of "countering the insurgency," turning colour-coded villages on the operations map from hostile-red to smile-and-wave green. Reluctant-amber at the very least. "We're building a nation, and if we pitch our vision to enough people, we can all go home." You wouldn't think a village's atmosphere was something to stake your life on, but senior guys tell you they can feel it in the air when something's about to go haywire. And sure enough, one village pegged as "bad juju" is where you see your first IED. At a bend in the road, they blow your lead truck sideways. A volcanic *boom*. Like planet Earth is sentient and has decided to knock you off its belly. Trucks are spaced in such a way that you see the blast before its *oom*-like report reaches your place in the convoy. This one-second delay feels like a slip in the veil of consciousness; us humans acting too crazy for the gods knitting our reality to keep up. Of course, in the heat of it, you're not pontificating the speed of sound or drawing metaphors—you're just scared shitless.

The dust settles and thankfully it's not a complex ambush. There's no ridgeline of fighters aiming rifles and rockets. There's no enemy to confront because whoever did this beat feet right after. Friends climbing out of the disabled truck massage their necks and blink away head trauma. Later they tell you the impact felt like falling in a dream, getting tipped out of a chair while napping and landing with a crash. The blast was big enough to topple a nearby building distraught pedestrians are calling a schoolhouse. It's a pile now. A building turned bucket, limp walls containing rubble. Thankfully, class was not in session, but still, the amassing villagers stare at you like this is all your fault—and not the direct action of the enemy, who could very well be standing amongst the gawkers.

"They could have placed this bomb anywhere," your platoon sergeant says, "hit us in the middle of nowhere. The fact they buried it next to a schoolhouse is very telling."

In attempts to ameliorate the mob, your platoon sergeant orders you to fill the blast crater, undo some of the damage caused by the people trying to kill you. You don't understand what difference this could make, and the task is excruciating in thirty pounds of equipment, bending for each scoop with a collapsible shovel that's about two feet long. For a brief second, though, you see stern faces begin to shift. *Maybe the Americans are helpful after all?*

This overt display of kindness might be worth it if you can soften their hearts while steeling your own.

Later that night, at the approximate time one of your battle-buddies is applying Tiger Balm to your spasming back, one of your high-school buddies back home is in a college dormitory with a naked nursing student bouncing on top of him. Later when this friend emails extensive notes of his exploits, envy causes you to curse his hedonistic freedom. There's a parallel universe where he's in your place and you're in his, the crippling student loans a worthy tradeoff for spending your best years uninhibited. But it's also the case that hard times create strong men—and that's still what you aim to be.

Your friend post-scripts his escapade by promising to send a picture next time. You reply:

Cool story, bro. I saw an elementary school get blown up today...

You don't bother telling him the school was empty—because fuck him.

Your platoon sergeant is smart for a grunt; also a bit of a weirdo. He reads scripture from several religious traditions and spends his mornings perched in a lawn chair by the noisy generators, staring off at nothing in particular. This sergeant, let's call him Lerner, offers an alternative narrative about Afghanistan than what's being peddled back home.

"Many Taliban fighters are former war orphans," he tells you. "Kids whose only means of education was austere doctrine."

Maybe this is why Lerner seems distracted following the schoolhouse bombing, solemn and more withdrawn than usual. While everyone else cheers that no children were harmed, he seems to mourn the loss of something more poetic. Something grander and harder to name than tiny dead bodies pinned under debris.

You don't fully grasp the context behind his orphan remark—and how could you, you're only eighteen. Your expertise lies in beating *The Legend of Zelda*. But through the natural osmosis that comes with immersion, small fragments of a larger mosaic are making themselves known. An interconnected saga that seems to stretch back endless generations beyond recorded history.

The platoon stumbles upon a burnt-out Russian tank, for instance, and although you're well aware of events in the eighties, seeing a live artifact feels anachronistic. Macabre even. This decaying machine dumped in a bright prairie of wildflowers connotes something only Lerner seems to pick up on. An omen intimating a rift in the space-time continuum. Like how you saw the IED before hearing it. You see the hull of a tank, and it's only later that your brain registers its full significance.

Driving away from the tank is also when you witness your second IED. This one even closer, louder, the sound delay less noticeable, like a dubbed film instead of warped physics. Four friends sustain injuries bad enough for CASEVAC. Broken ankles and dislocated knees. You wait around for the *whop-whop-whop* of a Black Hawk, and after the injured take to the skies your platoon feels even more vulnerable. Everyone will have to pull more weight.

Some of the boys from second platoon are circled up around a burn barrel debating the Big Bang hypothesis. You say you're unconvinced, and they look at you like you've been spending too much time with Lerner. You counter by saying you've never known an explosion to create, only to destroy, and with friends so recently injured the statement halts conversation.

"Did you know the theorist behind the Big Bang was a Catholic priest?" says Lerner out of nowhere. He joins the circle, and no one knows how to respond to a high-ranking NCO shooting the breeze with lowly privates. All eyes divert respectfully toward the fire.

Spring is in the air, and the warming weather is putting everyone at greater risk. Fighting season is yet another feature of the conflict you've been forewarned about. It was slightly amusing at first: the enemy's warfighting capacity grinds to a halt for . . . snow.

"But why not?" says Lerner. "They're in it for the long haul. We're in it for the we-don't-know-yet haul."

Now the snow is melting, and the uptick in violence has everyone on edge. Last week you helped Lerner treat a sucking chest wound on an Afghan soldier. One more element of war rigorously prepared for. You know what to do, in theory. Seal the wound and stab an airway between the victim's third and fourth intercostal space. What they don't tell you is the hissing sound or the blueness to the face suggesting death has already occurred and it will take a cosmic act, such as bending space-time, to adjust course.

You try and bend space time. Why the fuck not. A man's life is at stake.

You'd think the rib bones of a foot soldier from a third world country would be easy to demarcate, but after cutting away his fatigues you're met with a healthy slab of pectoral obscured by pink bubbles pooling at the entry wound. Fortunately, Lerner ignores radio commands long enough to do the hard part for you, as swift and effortlessly as someone punching a straw through a big gulp lid.

The man is spared at the cost of your shrinking confidence.

A week later, a nervous breakdown sends your favorite gaming buddy away for psychiatric care. *That's an option?* you wonder, and Lerner pulls you aside for a pep talk. Instead of calling your friend a coward—bidding good riddance to an eighteen-year-old PFC who couldn't stomach fighting season—instead of this, Lerner tries a different tact.

"Imagine an army unburdened by the psychological toll of war," he says. "How would they know when to stop?"

He offers another parable on his laptop, footage of a recent drone strike. A bird's-eye view pixelated, our world filtered through a digital lens. You see an enemy truck engulfed in black shroud, and when the smoke pulls away— like a magician's trick—the truck is gone.

"And what do you feel?" asks Lerner.

Nothing.

"Me neither."

Not so, you both agree, when you were treating the soldier with the sucking chest wound. That's why what we're doing here matters.

You tell him how you can't stop thinking about the two IEDs. The first one bad, the second one worse. It's like the path you're on is destined to end with a third and final bang, and you're trying to calculate if the looming risk is worth the final vision you have for yourself: someone tough, someone tested, someone damaged enough to understand the nature of reality—the good-versus-evil tug-of-war inside every beating heart.

Lerner nods. He too has spent a great deal of time pontificating the burdens and benefits of fighting terrorism; he's on the same path as you, only further down the road. The attention he's paid his life has instilled much wisdom. He talks; you listen. *Should you be taking notes?*

"An IED is every soldier's dread," he starts. "The same with being shot by a sniper: suddenly dropping on patrol like God is playing *Eeny, meeny, miny, moe.* The truth is you don't really know what to be afraid of until you see it in real time. And the things you can't see, can only expect, gnaw at you the most.

"Maybe this never-ending saga was fraught from day one. Who cares if this country is ruled by fanatics—can't we just boost our defenses at home and call it good? Even if we find some modicum of success here, we can't do one hundred percent good one hundred percent of the time. Maybe the only reasonable thing to do—when challenged by the insurmountable—is to tap out. Call it quits. Hey man—at least we tried, right? We'd only be the latest empire to stumble at the foot of these mountains.

"That's a valid reality we can choose to live in. But there also exists another story. About a school being bombed. About village leaders working with us to identify those responsible, providing actionable intel. About a night raid being organized as we speak. What I mean is, right now—sandwiched between shades of right and wrong, failure and doubt—we can solve this one problem. Go after a bonafide bad guy. Forget what history has to say decades later. In this moment—can you think of anything more important?"

His soliloquy pumps you up; you remember why you joined the Army in the first place. To become the ultimate *you*. There's just one lingering question. One final reluctance you can't seem to shake. Something you've been losing sleep over.

Is it very loud, you ask, getting blown up?

You thought your question silly and expected Lerner to laugh. He doesn't laugh. He tells you point-blank that *no*, a direct IED is silent, which feels like a lie. Survivors of the first IED aren't helpful either. They're uncertain. They hadn't thought about it before. "I don't know. I don't recall hearing a noise," one guy says, suspicious of his own syntax.

Trying to countenance the purported silence behind an explosion is when you decide you'll never understand how the world works, and the best you can do is try to understand yourself. Admitting this, you're able to fall asleep that night. Fast and uninterrupted sleep. A time will come when good sleep is a precious commodity, your recent bouts of insomnia are an omen-wormhole interlinking present you to future you.

A sneak peek of your life to come.

It's revenge time for the schoolhouse bombing, and you're star-struck when the big dogs saunter through the ops center: elite commandos schlepping gear priced at double your own. This is what you aim to be, in the flesh. Men who glide through doorways. Men whose uniform patches say nothing about where they are from. Men who spend an ungodly amount of tax money on their trigger time. Sexy stuff. And so is their operation. Smooth and seamless violence, like an orchestrated play, ardently rehearsed and now delivered live.

Doors are brought down using controlled blasts. Captives are taken. One insurgent dumb enough to crouch in the corner with an AK is lit up before getting off a single round. They find damning evidence, your heroes, not just a do-it-yourself kit but an IED assembly line.

You watch all this through your MRAP's windshield,

sans popcorn, and once again remember why you joined the Army. Yeah, top-tier action, vicarious it may be, is better than casual sex in a college dorm. This shit is worth the emotional scars of deploying. The action is over before it begins, but the sense of purpose afterwards is sheer ecstasy. Shared by one and all. A contact high from surviving the dangers of a bonafide combat operation. You have actually seen the Taliban, probably. Done more within your limited means than a great number of deployed troops can claim. It's such a climactic moment in the narrative you're constructing about yourself, you secretly wonder if all that's left is the denouement, when you pack it up and go back home. Of course, the next day after the movie-esque raid is just another day reset to boring status-quo. Year-long deployments are the perfect span of time to convince someone that things are happening for a reason. If there's a historical arc progressing, you can't detect it. Right now, the highs, the lows, are all subjective to your point of view. And your point of view hinges on who you think you are, or who you want to become.

One day, you begin to worry that to everyone back home—to the cosmic forces of the universe—the war retracted out is just white noise. A bunch of *stuff* that's happening in the background. To a disinterested third-party species, ant colonies locked in an aggressive battle would only look like bugs crawling in the dirt. But try saying that to a captured ant who's about to lose his head to razor-sharp mandibles.

During a smoke break, you share your thoughts with Lerner. It takes a couple of tries before he fully understands your half-baked teenage philosophizing. He takes a drag of his cigarette, exhales.

"What you tell yourself about Afghanistan, now or decades later, is for your benefit and no one else's."

Again, his words are elusive, if not downright contradictory to his earlier speech about purpose through microcosmic action. He does cause you to wonder what your future self will say when you're no longer so invested in the identity of *Soldier*. But right now, that's not a hypothetical you can devote much energy to because a new mission has just been planned. The same elite crew from the night raid needs your help on yet another capture or kill mission.

Your task is to cordon a village, set a perimeter so the bad guy doesn't escape. If you're the OR nurse prepping for an extraction, well now, here comes the surgeon. Seal Team whatever riding in on dune buggies. Guns pointing in all directions. "That's cool as shit!" your platoon agrees. "Why can't we have dune buggies?"

Lerner rolls his eyes. It doesn't take a lifer to know the constant visibility of conventional forces would make dune buggies too soft a target. A veritable *brah-brah-brah* deathtrap. One IED could probably take out three. Thankfully, the MRAP you're driving was built to withstand such a blast.

Once again, the Captain-America clones are a pleasure to work with. Everything just goes right for them. This one was too easy. Bad guy caught. No violence necessary. He woke to commandos hovering over his bed, end of story.

Afterwards, their team leader jokes with Lerner before bidding you all adieu, slapping the MRAP's fender like he just sold the darn thing to you. They ride outside the village where a Chinook helicopter waits to carry them, and their dune buggies, back to bed.

God that's cool. Unfortunately, you'll have to take the long way home.

It's a road you've driven countless times before, which puts your mind on autopilot. *Complacency kills*, they so often say. Keep your head on a swivel. Hard to keep these things in mind on month 11 of a 12-month deployment.

So, yes, this IED is for you. The biggest of them all.

You drive on top of it and—*boom*.

Probably the single-most overused word for describing explosions. Not inaccurate, though, like say, when viewing a three-hundred-pound IED from an approximate distance of two hundred meters. Yeah, it makes a *boom*. Similar with the visuals: if there wasn't so much dust and flame, your MRAP launching skyward—when viewed from a distance—would almost resemble a monster truck artfully flipping at a demolition rally.

This explosion, however, is not viewed from a two-hundred-meter distance. This explosion is absorbed from a zero-meter distance. From this perspective, an incalculable amount of kinetic power assaults your body at multiple resting points. Your feet, yes, but your trunk absorbs the crux of it all. In that regard, body armor is more a hindrance than help. The density of your plate carriers allowing no outlet for the upward ascending energy to escape.

Still, perhaps more interesting than inside the vehicle is what occurs inside your mind's eye. Your immediate vision fractures into something shrouded in twilight. Like blinking and finding yourself dreaming of the last thing you saw. Taking in life with your spirit, not with your eyes.

After the dust settles, your body slumps preternaturally, only a seatbelt between you and the steering wheel. You're dead. Welcome to death.

"He's gone," Lerner says after pressing under your jaw, and a strange mixture of fear and murderous rage fills the smokey compartment. It's just the emotion needed to put broken bodies into motion. Anyone in the vicinity who is not coalition forces would do well to stay out of M4 range right about now.

Wait, no, Lerner was finally wrong about something, because you return to life right around the time your friends are escaping via the gunner's hatch. Your time on the other side was brief but euphoric. No visuals of hell or divine revelations. No anything, really. No ill-will toward anyone.

No anxiety or pangs of identity. Only an envelopment, perhaps, *by that love that moves the sun and other stars.*

Your MRAP door pries open, and they carry you away right as the gas tank ignites. A MEDVAC bird is en route, so you don't get to stay for the full barbecue, only long enough to look beyond the medic offering sips of water and realize that the burning MRAP reminds you of something. *But what?* You're too punch-drunk and in too much pain to pair a memory with the déjà vu suffusing your sternum. Later when you realize the answer, it'll almost make you gasp. Like a word you couldn't think of, and only after you've stopped probing does the answer become painfully obvious. In front of you this whole time.

You'll also strain yourself trying to recall if you heard a sound. The bomb went off and . . . *it was silent, wasn't it?* Just like Lerner claimed. No burst eardrums to suggest otherwise.

Though when you revisit the IED in your dreams, a sound does accompany the blast. Not *boom* like you might expect, but ŌM.

ŌM. The sound credited in several religions with bringing life into this universe. Now a sound associated with birthing you into your ultimate self. Congratulations! You're not the action hero you'd envisioned; you have nightmares about losing your rifle in front of the first sergeant, and the titanium rods bracing your spine cap athletic ability. The tradeoff is you've been scarred with an indelible sense of spirituality. Although this world may never make sense, you've seen—felt more apt—something existing elsewhere. And just as a wise man once said in soliloquy how it's better to ground your identity on action you can take and not how others view you, so too will that ethereal sense of elsewhere always remain a lofty thing to consider when learning to be you.

Love
in the Time of Combat Injuries

WALTER REED HAD A BAD REP by the time I medevac'd there. A shocking exposé had uncovered gross inadequacies. Soldiers were allegedly dying in vermin-infested hospital rooms, crying out to a nurses' station that either couldn't hear them or didn't care. Hard for me to imagine, because when I rolled through in 2010, it was a little annex of heaven on an otherwise tedious Earth.

Maybe this was because of the mass opioids swimming through my system—morphine on-demand. Maybe because the staff were the kindest, most upbeat people I'd ever met—picture Bob Ross coming to check your vitals. Or maybe it was Hannah.

We met in an elevator of all places. I don't know whether to call it a meet-cute or a meet-ugly. I was celebrating sitting up for the first time in weeks. Finally, I'd been fitted with a TLSO back brace and transferred to my very own wheelchair. Freedom of mobility was extraordinary after spending weeks wondering if I'd ever walk again. Especially after touring the hospital grounds and seeing how some of the other patients were fairing. 2010 was the deadliest year in Afghanistan, but at least I had all my limbs. No disfiguring burns or brain injuries rendering me permanently altered. Just a couple of burst fractures to my spine. And when feeling came back to my legs, I knew my injuries were something I could handle. Easily. Well, maybe not *easily*. I did have a Foley catheter shoved up my dick and things were mighty irregular on the other end, too. All that morphine had cemented my digestive tract. Milk of mag and other laxatives got things going, about the pace of a D.C. freeway at 1600 rush hour. I was lucky if I could squeeze something into a bedpan once a week. And whenever I could, it was always embarrassing to have to call one of the hot 2nd lieutenant nurses to come flush it down the toilet and wipe up after me. Like: *please, please, please,* I'd always pray hitting the call button, *send the jolly Puerto Rican guy, not the cute brunette with the southern accent.*

But Hannah wasn't a nurse. I'm not Hemingway, and this isn't a Nicholas Sparks story. At first sight, you could say I was struck by her beauty. More so, I was struck I could see her at eye level. The elevator opened and—bam! We were face-to-face . . . because she was in a wheelchair, too.

"Uh, right," is what she said, realizing I was rolling aboard. We performed a wheelchair dance to allow for us both.

"Similar predicament," I said, parallel parking beside her.

"Looks that way."

That awkward elevator silence usually mollified by jazz music arose. I used it to study her in my peripheries, pretending at one point to yawn and stretch my neck for a full look. Her curly ponytail had streaks of chestnut, an artisanal blend of dark and milk chocolate. I remember thinking: can you dye your hair in the Army? I still don't know the answer. The rest of her felt very civilian as well. Reflective running shorts, a polychrome Coldplay t-shirt, and a jingling charm bracelet that interfered with wheelchair operation.

Her missing left leg—that was the most military thing

about her. Seeing it caused me to squirm in sympathy, so I diverted my gaze to her other leg which was olive-toned and muscular and smooth-looking, causing a very different type of unease.

The piss bag by my side made me feel naked—the tube looping out of my shorts and outing me as a man who could not properly relieve himself—as if my vulnerable insides were now on the outside and exposed to the world. I hoped it didn't stink. A mental note was made to bring a blanket on my next corridor adventure.

"This is my floor," I said when the doors opened.

"Mine too."

Military-instilled chivalry demanded she exit first, despite me being better situated. Thankfully, common sense won out. Rather than play bumper cars, I elected to make space by leaving. As I did, my tiny front wheel sunk into the gap between floor and elevator.

She suppressed a laugh. A sympathetic face that seemed to ask: first time?

"I think I need an adult," I said.

The elevator doors slammed into me only to reopen. I tried popping a wheelie but to no avail. "I guess I'll holler for the nurses' station."

"No, I got you." She executed a quick turn, locked her wheels, and then gently pulled on my backrest. "Okay—go, go, go!"

I did and was freed.

I thanked her in the lobby.

"You'll get the hang of it."

This begged me to ask how long she'd been here.

"Longer than I'd like," was her response.

I tried my friendliest smile and extended a hand.

"Sergeant Fischer."

She looked but didn't take.

"Maybe we can just *not* with the whole rank thing," she said, explaining her belief that Walter Reed's informal ecosystem made for a smoother convalescence. "Call me Hannah." She offered her hand, charm bracelet rattling.

"Jake. Glad to know ya."

We exchanged room numbers, and she said to visit anytime, just down the hallway.

"We can brew coffee, or tell war stories, or drag race our wheelchairs," she said.

And when she turned to go, all I could think was: is five minutes from now too soon?

We fell into a rhythm of sorts, encouraged by the highly structured yet stale environment in which we lived. Every morning I'd wheel my ass down to her room for French press coffee, much richer than what they served in the cafeteria. I learned she had been a schoolteacher before joining the Marine Corps, which came as a double surprise. I would have pegged her for Air Force. Parents from her third-grade class banded together and bought her that jingly bracelet she wore as a going-away present, one charm from each of her twenty students. I didn't ask how she'd managed to hold onto it through war, a combat injury, to the here and the now at Walter Reed. But her charm bracelet story was the most wholesome thing I'd heard since . . . ever. She laughed at that one.

"Though not a good-luck token," I said.

She laughed at that, too. "Oh, I don't know. I've still got my right leg.

Hannah loved teaching, it turned out. "Too much," she said. "I realized I could sit back and do this for the rest of my life, no problem. So, I joined the Marine Corps."

"Naturally."

She grinned. "It scared me that the only life I'd know would be the one I started when I was twenty-three."

"Yeah—no. I totally get it," I said, trying not to reveal how self-conscious I felt. Twenty-three was my exact age. And the only life I'd known was the one I started at eighteen.

Best judgment put her at least four to eight years older than me. Certainly someone I would be allowed to have feelings for in the civilian world, though in the military there was always the question of rank, which she still refused to disclose. A sergeant dating a staff sergeant might not look so odd. A sergeant dating an officer—don't even think about it. I wasn't an air-headed romantic—these are just the scenarios your mind runs in a painkiller-induced fugue. Outside of these bedside fantasies, we were just two plainclothes people who enjoyed each other's company. I convinced myself not to have any expectations beyond that. Two fit, attractive people who just so happen to understand the unique disposition of the other. We could relate. Chat about the growing pains, phantom pains, and-or psychological pains of being a wounded warrior. For instance: I could gripe about the Foley tube I'd finally—mercifully—had removed, and she could view me as more than just a limp, watery-eyed victim.

"I sympathize," she said. "That's an unusual experience for a male. Just be glad you'll never have to deliver a baby from the same area."

And what could I say in return? *Oh, you can't understand—you only lost a leg*! In this way, we held each other accountable. Casting a life-preserver that kept us both from sinking.

"You want kids?" I asked, because I'm incapable of holding a nuanced conversation.

She practically cackled. "Can you imagine me hobbling after a two-year-old?"

"Well, I mean—you'll have a prosthesis, yeah?"

"I suppose that's true. Currently I'm focused on the next

step now—no pun intended. Not the next step five years from now."

Sooooo . . . She's twenty-eightish? Can't be much older than thirty.

She ran a hand through her hair. "Let's just say I'll have an interesting dating life when I get back on my feet. *Foot.* And by interesting, I mean nonexistent."

"That's what you predict?"

"That's what I know. I'm not stupid, I saw the look on your face when you first saw me."

A few starts, stops, and stutters, and I confirmed it's true—she was very startling. That was my first reaction. "But then I saw you in those running shorts and thought: Damn, nice legs. Er. Leg. Very toned."

Her eyes narrowed. "If you had a Foley in right now—I'd rip it out."

I crossed my arms over my groin. "Oof. You don't hear a comment like that," I said. "You feel it."

And when the nurse came in because we were laughing so loud, we both said sorry and popped smoke to the cafeteria where we could be as loud as we wanted.

There was no shortage of visitors at Walter Reed: B-list celebrities, sports icons, politicians angling for a human-interest selfie. A cohort of Gold Star moms dropped by my room one afternoon and stayed till nightfall, ultimately surprising me with an X-box, a small tradition they'd all started together.

"A whole damn X-box!" I said to Hannah.

"Wow, not half an X-box?"

I told her not to joke. It was humbling being in their presence. They reminded me of my mom, who had stayed a week in D.C. when I first arrived. I'll never forget being combat wounded, doped up on morphine in Germany, then handed a phone to notify my family. I was so scared. Mom would kill me if she found out I got hurt. Worse, it would kill her. A heart attack over the phone. It rang a few times and I thought I was safe—I could mask the truth in voicemail. *Just a few small fractures. Certainly not a broken spine if that's what you're thinking.* Of course, she answered, and all I could think to say was, "*Heeey,* Mom . . . Is Dad around?"

So I could hardly look these Gold Star moms in the eye, knowing what they'd been through.

Hannah had a different philosophy.

"Just imagine how hard it was for them to *face you.*"

Oh. Well . . . fuck. She was probably right.

Powerlessness was often the hardest thing for me to accept. *This is temporary*, being my daily mantra. Soon my spine would be strong enough to support my weight, and they'd let me stand up again. Until then I felt feeble. More a nuisance than anything. The thing is: I'm a shallow man. Take away my powers of physicality and what am I left with? What's my identity? *Army Sergeant turned Wounded Warrior.* I didn't want my woundedness to define me. Problem is, you have no choice—that's how people view you. *Yes, yes, I'm down here in this chair, but I used to be a real badass!* Most of the time, I secretly gushed over the warm attention. Except when it struck home just how incapable I really was. Like the first time I saw Hannah doing physical therapy.

With further surgeries pending, they couldn't give her crutches for fear she'd fall. Yet it was worth the risk to get her up on those PT walking lanes to stretch her good leg and put weight on it.

She was standing and doing dips, much against the wishes of her physical therapist who hovered ready to catch her.

"Holy cow, are you taller than me?" I asked.

"That depends," she said, "how tall are you?"

"Five-ten."

"I'm only five-nine."

Phew.

"And a half."

Goddamn it. They said I lost a quarter inch of height after surgery, so that put us nearly neck and neck. I don't know why I fretted over these things. Maybe when your identity has already taken a blow you try and reclaim what small vanities you can. I wondered if Hannah felt the same about anything.

The therapist guided her to a chair, and I wished it were me. I wanted to stand strong and upright and catch her if she fell. All I could do was be her buddy. And like a groveling kid brother I asked if she wanted to watch the movie *Avatar,* which neither of us had seen due to being deployed.

She said yes and came to my room for a change of scenery. Also, I had the X-box.

"Come in—come in!" I said, "hors d'oeuvres start at five. Can I get you a glass of chardonnay?"

Her hair was down. She kept fidgeting with loose strands, tucking them behind ears that were pierced with gold hoops.

We laughed out loud when the movie's protagonist turned out to be a Marine in a wheelchair.

"He's fucked up like us!" she said, pointing.

Throughout the movie I wrestled with the urge to reach for her hand, but the right moment never came, and I couldn't decide if I should try casually or make a permission-based thing out of it. Then my back started burning from sitting up all day and a nurse had to come transfer me into bed. Suffice to say, whatever dim-lit mood we started with was spoiled. The nurse informed me that I would be upgrading to a walker soon. This seemed even more emasculating than a wheelchair. With a wheelchair there's a relaxed dignity: a speed and grace in zipping around the hospital corridors.

In a walker I would become a hundred-year-old millennial, struggling once again with a basic mode of human existence.

We both loved *Avatar*. "And fuck that crazy colonel for picking on the aliens!" Actually, that part annoyed us. Not quite disillusioned with the military just yet, it was hard not to see ourselves as the villain. But we were also the protagonist.

"Would you be a tall blue alien on another planet?" I asked.

"Sign me up."

"What about Earth?"

"Earth's overrated. We have a beautiful world here, though most never see it. Too busy in cubicles. I want to soar on pterodactyls surrounded by limitless colour and splendor."

This comment evolved into a discussion of morphine. We both agreed: it was simultaneously a cold and hot sensation. It's possible for the human body to replicate this in extreme scenarios. Like when sleep-deprived, your body pulses cold to power you down. Or when kissing someone on a first date, your body sends heat to make you feel good. These are natural drips you're capable of, whereas morphine is a false but steady flow.

"Let's try and simulate morphine," I said. "We'll stay up all night—kissing."

I could hardly believe the words escaped my mouth and was terrified of the power she now had to either gently diffuse the suggestion or explode it altogether. How awful it would be to pass her in the hallways and it be awkward instead of something to look forward to. And it sounds young-adultish to describe how giddy-relieved I felt when she unlocked her wheelchair and brought herself closer to my bed.

"It's certainly worth a try," she said.

"For science," I said, sitting up.

"For science."

I'll spare gushy details, except it's worth noting that her charm bracelet by my ear sent tingles throughout my body. And similar to how I started this foolhardy make-out sesh, something inward compelled me to press pause. *Is this okay*, my mind raced. *Should we be more grown-up about this?* The truth is there is something impossibly immature about nascent love at any age. So when I pulled away and asked, "What are we doing?" her playful response of "We're convalescing" was all the justification I needed. After we were again separated by the squeaky cart of a nurse about to enter on rounds, I went to sleep soaring on something other than opioids.

Like every great romcom, there comes a time where the couples are pitted against each other by asinine conflict. Usually due to a white lie, job loyalties, or soft trickery that the audience has seen cooking since scene one.

What happened with Hannah was I had just been trained on how to use a walker and wanted to shuffle by her room and impress her with my elevated mobility. However, instead of Hannah, there was a custodial worker tidying up her room, which Hannah would have loathed the thought of. When this staff member saw me, she was so polite and humble—clearly a civilian doing her best to keep up with military formalities. "Captain Reese is out for physical therapy," she said.

I nodded and turned to leave. I couldn't let this kindhearted worker know she had just shattered the make-believe world I had grown so comfortable in.

Hannah was a fucking captain.

I roamed the halls, unsure of what to do with this information. Should I be mad at her? Or is that a reaction mimicked from movies. If I do get mad, could I be penalized for insubordination—*ha!*

I decided I was more impressed than anything. Staff here knew she was a captain, and I doubted they were blind to us sneaking and flirting around. Still, it felt different when she wheeled toward me grinning from here to Baghdad.

"Look at you!" she said, and then stopped, sensing my reluctance. "What's wrong?"

I executed a textbook salute. "Good afternoon, Ma'am."

She sighed. "You're going to get weird now, aren't you."

"You've got some big balls, you know that."

"Yes, they're Marine Corps issue."

"Because you have the most to lose here, Captain."

"Seriously? You really think they'd court martial the one-legged woman? Dress blues, the whole circus, wheeled before my superiors. Can you even explain the rules on fraternization?"

"I know it's not allowed."

"Jake, are we in a combat zone? Am I in command of troops? Or am I in a hospital missing eight pounds of leg and about to start the long, depressing process of being med-boarded out of the Marine Corps?"

If this were a romcom, it would make more sense to play-up this dispute. Drag it on so the audience sits and wonders if we will or if we won't. That's not what happened. We were both adults. We both knew the risks. And it was the easiest thing in the world to toss these concerns behind us and carry on. I worked in the odd joke now and then. Like, after we discovered I could grip her wheelchair handles and she could be my walker, she'd say: "Take us outside," and I'd reply: "Aye, Captain." Or after the nurse would finish with rounds, Hannah would command from bed to "Close the door," and I'd reply: "Yes, Ma'am."

So no, our gentle rule-breaking was merely a speedbump on our road to intimate connection. We adored each other, as people often say when they can't admit the L-word.

In the end it was my sudden orders back home that split us apart.

I was well enough to fly, which means I was well enough to vacate Walter Reed. It was now the responsibility of a Warrior Transition Unit to determine my fate. Either med-board like Hannah or reclass to an office MOS less intensive on the spine. On our final night, I hobbled into her room around 0100 and a bemused doctor found us cuddled asleep a few hours later. Apparently, we were talk-of-the-town at the nurses' station.

We tiptoed around defining what we were. Neither of us quite ready to admit how much we meant to each other. So, we had this misfired Casablanca good-bye. Something I regretted immediately upon boarding the aircraft.

"In my most vulnerable moment—you were exactly the goofy guy I needed," I think she said, touching my face.

In *all* of my moments she was exactly the headstrong girl I needed, I wished I would have said in return. Instead, I fumbled. At a genuine loss for words. Walter Reed was the only reason we connected, right? We were incompatible out in the real world. Here she was stating otherwise, reducing her rank and baring her soul—it's so clear now that we had surmounted barriers. If I had more time to think things through, I probably would have recognized she was reaching out for me to reciprocate, allowing me to take an equal initiative.

But I failed. I stared like a deer in headlights, until her warm expression morphed into something blank and shy.

I should have begged to exchange emails. I should have tattooed hers on my forearm.

"Well, take care of yourself," she said.

And half an hour later when I'm locked in a transport litter on a C-130, I imagined ripping out of my confines, standing and sprinting off the tail ramp to tell her how much

I love her. We'd kiss and kiss, and she'd give me her charm bracelet and I'd offer my dog tags: a down payment on our plans to one day reunite. But all I could do was lie prone and laugh-cry about how an airplane is always involved in these situations.

This was right before everyone and their mother joined social media, mind you. So, a few years later, when everyone is online and personal information is no longer sacrosanct, as I lie awake stationed at a starry Bagram Airfield, the thought sprints across my mind to crack open my laptop and type Hannah Reese into the search bar. After doing this, the screen loads and a rush of something more actionable than nostalgia fills me.

Her profile shows a figure on a paddleboard. I confirm it's her by the titanium leg standing firm and glinting below the knee. You're not supposed to get prostheses wet, so there she goes again breaking the rules. My message is already taking shape when I click on her picture. Is that you, Captain Reese? But when her profile opens to a collage of photos chronicling her life outside the Marine Corps, I freeze. Something swells inside me, then it withers and dies. It's not pain or disappointment I feel, it's my soul acknowledging that I'm not messaging an old friend and lover, I'm a voyeur spying on someone I no longer know.

Here's Hannah in a white dress.

Here's Hannah's newborn son.

Here's a clip of Hannah chasing him at the beach.

And it fills my heart to see—she's keeping up just fine.

THE PHANTOM RANK

THE WARRIOR TRANSITION UNIT was where they sent you to learn the high art of being a broke dick. A convalescent home for wounded and-or defective soldiers. About half the people here had at least one decent story, otherwise they wouldn't be here. Then there were the other half who would be here regardless. That special breed of warrior who sprains his ankle shooting hoops, or whose back gives out on one of those pesky garrison ruck marches, or—heaven forbid—soldiers who claim debilitating PTSD from a lone rocket that strikes outside of Bagram.

Soldiers with bonafide combat injuries were usually more chipper than the others. They had pep in their step—if they could step—and would look you in the eye, grin, and explain in simple conversation how they ended up here. There was nothing for them to be ashamed of. No reason for them to trail off or change the subject to avoid detailing their anti-climactic origins bereft of a combat experience. I belonged to the proud camp of combat wounded and was treated like royalty. So did Wally. He too had a Purple Heart and an assortment of robot parts such as plates and screws. But when asked about his injuries, he would always shy away, utter a few choice phrases, and behave with the same fleeting confidence of someone faking it. Peculiar, given that it only took one look to surmise he'd been seriously fucked up overseas.

We were paired together as roommates—as battle buddies—because of a shared combat injury. A calcaneus fracture, or a shattered heel in plain English. A brutal fucking injury requiring reconstructive surgery and guaranteeing a lifetime of impaired balance and mobility—and that's best-case-scenario. My super-fracture was the left, and thanks to hot yoga, and a still-functioning right heel, I would eventually rediscover my regular athletic self. But Wally had two of these injuries. He would walk around in giant boots for extra cushioning, wobbly—yet rigid—and in a fair amount of pain. I knew 'cause I was experiencing the same. But to others, I don't think he let on just how much he was hurting. When passing on the sidewalk, he would smile, pick up his pace a little, but soon return to hobbling like someone walking barefoot on gravel. Everyone liked Wally. Everyone but me, I'm ashamed to say.

Barracks back then were split bedrooms sandwiching a kitchen and common area. I was tidying up our shared bathroom in anticipation of a room inspection when he came lumbering in wearing a vibrant Muscle Beach tank top, even though we were stationed in the dreary Pacific Northwest.

He was tan and imposing and introduced himself with a wide smile and a balmy handshake. I can't remember what he said exactly, I was too distracted by the series of oblong pink scars that decorated his upper pecs and arms.

"Holy shit, dude. Are those from the IED?"

"Ha-ha, *no*," he bellowed. "These are from a knife fight. Before I joined the Army."

He then gave a full report of how he had earned these

badges. It was curious he would give a play-by-play of a civilian knife fight but eschew all particulars of his IED injuries. An IED put me here, too. If there was anyone who could relate. . .

But all he said on the topic was: "Yep. Knife wounds. Then I got blown the fuck up in a Stryker. If I can get myself shot, I'll hit the trifecta—ha-ha-ha!"

He had a quick breathy energy to match his laugh.

"Listen," he said. "Now that we're roomies, I figure we ought to have each other's back."

"That's the general idea."

"Like if a guy needs a Q-tip," he said, plucking one from my tiny glass container on the sink before jamming it in his ear. "He can take one without asking."

"Be my guest."

Thanks, man!" He clapped me on the shoulder. "Help yourself to any of my stuff."

He dropped the Q-tip—now coated in wax—in the sink and wandered off to his private quarters where sounds of an intense videogame battle emanated. I shuddered moving the Q-tip from sink to receptacle.

Opening the fridge, I realized neither of us had any food. And "his stuff" constituted obnoxiously large containers of protein powder overtaking most of the counter space.

Whenever dressed in ACUs, a new Wally would emerge. A man less boisterous and more stoic than the roommate I knew. It was as if by wearing the flag and unit patches on his sleeves he was still a part of an ongoing mission; lives were at stake, so he better comport himself accordingly. *This* Wally, I would have been proud to serve with. But this persona was a holdover. An echo. A lingering fragment of Wally's nobler self. Because the first thing I noticed, aside from his shoulders pulled back with greater confidence, was the absence of rank upon his chest. At first, I didn't have the heart to ask what he'd been busted down for. All I knew was our section sergeant, SSG Vo, still referred to him as "Sergeant Wallace." A nod of respect, or perhaps an appeal to the side of Wally who still wanted to walk and talk Army. Most people get demoted for stupid shit: smoking pot, going AWOL, a DUI. When this happens whatever devotion they have to their military bearing usually dies along with their careers. Not Wally, though. He still had pride donning the superhero suit. Even as an E-1.

Eventually, rumors surrounding his demotion began to circulate the barracks like any other gossip, only with Wally there were several conflicting reports.

He punched an LT downrange, one person claimed. This one was somewhat plausible.

No, he was in a gun-smuggling scheme, said someone else. *M4s going straight to motorcycle clubs.* This one would be downright criminal.

There were demotion stories about the sergeant major's daughter, as there are on any military base. Another person said he smashed a Stryker through an Afghan residence—an improvised combat maneuver, perhaps?

Then a sad version emerged in which he'd gone AWOL after the death of a friend. The weird thing about this one was it had a conclusion. Apparently, he was found at an ANA checkpoint living with Afghan troops. Eating with them, sleeping in their barracks—even taking turns pulling guard duty.

"They're all lies," Wally said with a cheeky smile.

"Why are there so many?" I asked.

"Because I started them."

Why would someone do such a thing? If you knew Wally, you wouldn't have to ask. You'd know why, even if you couldn't articulate it.

Another thing Wally and I had in common was a gorgeous physical therapist we were both hopelessly in love with. We called her Doc, like a medic, and started announcing our pending appointments as if they were something to brag about.

"Later, buddy. I'm off to see Doc."

"Gah, you son of a bitch. I don't see her till next week."

We liked to joke about which one of us had better odds with her—us two defective soldiers with our combined 1.5 high school diplomas.

"I'm gonna use the GI Bill to become an FBI agent," I'd argue.

"But I'm using mine to pay for helicopter school," he'd counter.

"She seems like someone more attracted to danger over a big salary."

"What's more dangerous than flying Black Hawks?"

For what it's worth, I think he meant more to her as a patient than me.

One time we had back-to-back appointments. I was lounging outside the therapy mats but could hear their conversation. She had his boots off and was yanking and twisting at the ankles, range of motion tests she'd soon perform on my heel fracture.

"What's my prognosis?" I heard him say.

"You won't be running marathons anytime soon," she said.

"Can I still shoot, move, and communicate?"

I heard what sounded like a joint popping.

"*Do you*—do you still want to shoot, move, and communicate?" she asked, her voice somewhat inflected for delicate impact.

"I just thought if I heal up alright, I might still be of service."

I couldn't quite make out what she said in response.

Wally exited a few minutes later.

"Sup, pencil dick," he said to me.

"Fuck you, clown shoes," I said, smirking at his gaudy civilian boots that needed retying.

During my PT session, Doc posed the same question:

"Your heel is coming along nicely. Let me guess—you want to return to duty?"

"No, not me, Ma'am," I said with modest restraint to not sound privy to her conversation with Wally. "I'm trying to get out of here ASAP."

The way I saw it, the first IED had compromised my body. I didn't want to think about getting hit again. This didn't seem to be a concern for Wally. Even though, of the two of us, he was the worse off.

One morning, Wally didn't show for formation. A formation no more or less distinct than the countless other mornings at the WTU. SSG Vo counted us all up, noticed his absence and glared at me.

What? I wanted to say like an angsty teenager. *Am I my battle-buddy's keeper?*

Well, yeah, it turned out I was. Which would have made sense if we were about to deploy together. In our liminal world, it felt like every man for himself. We're here to get away from here. There were zero ramifications for failing to form a tight-knit bond; we wouldn't be saving each other's lives in combat anytime soon.

Vo walked me back to the barracks so I could let him in to perform a welfare knock on Wally's bedroom.

We found him curled in bed. An empty bottle of painkillers tipped over on his nightstand. Vo pushed past the fatigues, the old prosthetic boots and other detritus littering the floor and shook the living shit out of him. Not sure if this was good judgement because Wally shot up like Dracula—

like someone ready to rip Vo's throat out.

He played dumb when he saw who it was. "Wah. Did I miss formation?" he said, like it was simply a matter of a malfunctioning alarm clock.

It took some convincing, but Vo left believing Wally's prescription had finished on schedule. He claimed he only ever took the prescribed amount, but I suspected otherwise.

"I looked like a punk out in formation without you," I said.

"I'm sorry," he said. "I couldn't sleep last night—the pain was too much."

"Quit acting like a baby. I have the same injury. I don't take shit for it."

"Not that kind of pain."

This was something I wasn't ready to confront. Emotions were a language neither of us were very fluent in. Plus, he was so unwilling to talk about his circumstances, at least with me.

"All I'm saying is if you want to stay in the Army, you need to start acting like it, *Sergeant.*"

He stood and puffed up to his full, impressive height. "Who told you I want to stay in the Army?"

The sting of accusation caused me to squirm, thinking he was calling me out for eavesdropping on him and Doc.

"You did," I managed to say. "Black Hawk school, remember?"

His body seemed to deflate.

"Oh, yeah. People can learn to fly helicopters in the civilian world, too—am I right?"

"Of course, man. A solid career choice. Something positive to aim for."

I thought of clapping him on the shoulder. Right over one of his gnarly knife scars. But the whole brouhaha thing was more his department, so instead I gently excused myself from his personal space, shutting the door on him.

For the first time, it was quiet on his side of the barracks.

As the weeks in Army-career limbo ticked by, Wally became an increasingly elusive figure. Often heard but seldom seen. I was living with a specter who would occupy the bathroom on occasion or leave crumbs on the kitchen counter. He never missed another formation, and he seemed to be out more often than in. I laughed, thinking of myself as a jealous spouse, waiting up till breaking morning for a chance to interrogate him.

Just where have you been all hours of the night?

I can smell the booze from ten feet away, Wallace.

You think it's pleasant eating dinner alone?

That last one despite the fact we never really broke bread together, except once or twice sitting at the same DFAC table.

Next time I saw him, it was by accident. I was once again in Doc's waiting area outside the therapy mats. Someone was on the other side, crying. A measured yet hyperventilating noise.

Embrace the suck, loser.

I recalled the first few rounds of therapy I gnashed my teeth through—using happy thoughts, Doc's encouragement, and other such Zen techniques to mitigate the pain. Last thing I wanted was to become dependent on the opioids prescribed all too freely around here.

Next, I heard Mr. Weepy Eyes croak:

"It shouldn't have been me."

Tough cookies, it was you, I thought. *No one's gonna do your therapy for you—so get busy. There's no one better than Doc.*

I was motivating the fuck out of myself if no one else.

"I don't deserve it," the muffled voice said, to which I scoffed, shaking my head.

Leering with a wry smile at the sound of approaching footsteps, I wanted to lock eyes with whomever she was working with. The thought crossed my mind that this person could be seriously fucked up, missing limbs or badly burned; a signal from my kinder brain slapping my ego upside the head. I braced for a sudden wave of debilitating guilt but felt more confusion than anything when Wally rounded the corner.

"You good, man?" I asked, genuinely concerned. "I didn't know you had an appointment today."

"I didn't," he said, walking straighter than ever. "Just saying goodbye."

"Wait, you're leaving?"

"Funny thing about winter. The fighting stops and med-board paperwork starts to clear."

"Well—see you back at the place?" I called to him. He extended a thumbs-up on his way out the door.

Inside her cubicle, Doc was staring at a blank screen, gnawing on a pen cap. She spun around and smiled at me with those clear kaleidoscope blues.

"How's the pain today?"

"Zero," I said, even though it was really a three out of ten. The changing weather had permeated my tendons, now my heel clicked as I rolled out each step.

"That's good to hear. You're making excellent progress. But let's see if we can get even better than zero, shall we?"

Wally's protein containers were gone by the time I returned home. I thought he was too, until his bedroom door suddenly propped open, a tan and combat boot serving as door wedge. Inside was clean and squared away, a radical departure from the slovenly state he usually kept things in. He still had a week or so before clearing post; evidently, he wasn't wasting any time.

"So, what's next for you?" I asked.

He was sweeping dust bunnies to the center of his room. He stopped, touched the broomstick to his cheek, and said, "Thought about working at a fish processing plant up in Alaska. Twelve-hour days, a filet knife, and an endless conveyor belt of salmon."

"Oh," I said slightly taken back. "That sounds like a living hell."

"Exactly," his eyes grew wide. "But it's big money for hard work."

"What about helicopter school?"

Because of his demotion, Wally explained, he was receiving a *General Discharge*. A VA Disability, yes, but no GI Bill as punishment for his lack of honor.

I was incensed for him.

"You gotta fight that shit. There has to be an appeal process, right?"

"It's all good," he said nonplussed. "Save that hoity-toity college shit for the sons and daughters of people who earned it."

"But you did earn it!"

"I'll tell you what really pisses me off," he said, grinning, "you're gonna go get all college-educated and then one-up me with Rachelle."

Doc, he meant. Calling her anything else felt weirdly insubordinate.

"I don't know," I said. "I'm not on a first-name basis with her."

"Hm. Well, you still have time."

He went back to his sweeping.

A week later, I drove him to the train station. He exited his immaculate bedroom wearing full ACUs, the black beret already stretched across his scalp so his hands could manage two duffle bags.

He saw my eyes trail up and down his uniform and said: "I just want to wear it one last time. I'll change once we're off post."

"Wait one second."

I retreating to my desk, rifling through the drawer in search of a small token I had absolutely no use for. An E-5 patch. Chevrons I carefully aligned on his chest, pressing the Velcro with a small degree of ceremony. Standing back, I felt I was suddenly in the presence of authority.

"Where'd you get this," he asked.

"Bought it expecting a promotion board. Got blown up instead. Don't count your chickens, right?"

"Thanks," he said, picking at the patch's top corner, "but it's not my rank."

"You sure about that, Sergeant?"

I assumed parade rest. This may have been overkill. He laughed and swatted at me to knock it off, but we left the barracks with the rank still adorned.

SSG Vo stopped us in the lobby. He nodded approval at Wally's uniform. Gave a quick overhand right to his chest, making his promotion even more official. They exchanged numbers, shook hands. No hug, though. Hugs are reserved for people you bleed and die with. Vo was only a garrison sergeant to us.

Other soldiers and civilian staff came to say their goodbyes, their tone and mannerisms reserved and overly polite. It was usually a momentous occasion—getting the fuck out of the WTU. I think we all had our reservations about Wally.

We drove the long way off post. Waved to the MPs pulling guard duty. The access-control gate was still visible in the rearview mirror when Wally said, "Strange. I don't feel any different. It's just—I thought I might."

"You're a free bird." I elbowed his arm.

"Yeah. I guess I can go anywhere?"

I noticed he said it as a question, not a statement.

At the train station, Wally took the lead on our goodbye. One of those bro-ish handshake-hugs. An in-between. We hadn't fought together—but we shared a similar combat experience. We promised to *friend* each other online.

"Been real good being roomies with you," he said.

"Likewise."

We studied each other for a moment.

"Well, thanks for the ride." He turned toward the station.

"Anytime." Not sure why this ill-fitting word was the only thing that came to me.

Before I could buckle back in the driver's seat, Wally had spun around. Clenching his bags extra tight, he looked me in the eye and said:

"Hey man. We used to be something, yeah? Before we got hurt."

He was looking for validation, I thought. A final statement capping his military career.

"We still are," I called to him over the hood of my car.

He nodded like this was what he wanted to hear.

His train departed. A locomotive to be subsumed by a city too busy to register its arrival. In the same way Wally would be enveloped by a world indifferent to his existence.

Over the next year, he would drift along. I would leave the WTU shortly after. Many months would overlap in which we both lived in neighboring states. We *liked* each other's status updates and tossed around the idea of a reunion—half-hearted intentions used to fill a void in our online conversation. It became clear that outside of the military we didn't have very much in common. Then Wally stopped posting altogether. I would use my GI Bill to enroll in school. I would get engaged. And only after I had all but forgotten about Wally would I see his picture in the newspaper. The newspaper, of all fucking mediums. One on display as I waited for my fiancé—an aspiring veterinarian from community college—to finish paying at the self-checkout kiosk at our local grocery. It was his face on the front page that caught my eye. He looked healthy, happy, but the headline above him was anything but.

Decorated Army Veteran Dies by Suicide

"God fucking damn it!" I said and ripped the newspaper from its display stand. The frontpage was only an introduction. Loose newspaper fell to the floor as I searched for section B3. Ink rubbed onto my fingertips, and the lady at the customer-service counter eyed me warily.

The article explained in less than four hundred words what Wally himself refused to divulge.

Wally had been the sole survivor of a massive IED attack. A complex ambush if I had to guess from the newspaper's vague wording. He lost four friends that day. His sister, interviewed for the paper, speculated that "He was suffering from survivor's guilt. He missed the Army, too. He always said enlisting was the most positive thing he had done with his life."

I hadn't heard the term survivor's guilt before. Most problems those days all got shelved under a single blanket acronym. Soldiers suffering from a variety of demons all got the same treatment: a doggy bag of Prozac and a good-game slap on the ass.

I read the article thoroughly, though there were moments when I wanted to stop. Thankfully, the paper avoided fine details. I didn't want confirmation of how Wally ended his life. It was easy enough to guess—we all seem to pick the same quick familiar way. If I had to put a name to it, guilt was what I was feeling when my fiancé approached and saw me cross-referencing the newspaper with my iPhone. A torrent of memorials had flooded his online profile. Friends, family, fellow soldiers from the WTU—dozens of people paused their day to leave a comment on Wally's profile. SSG Vo seemed particularly devastated. His comment named all the fallen soldiers he had known; his final sentence ascribing

Wally to their ranks. Some comments were mad. Some were sad. Others, like myself, questioned if they could have done more, weighing every micro-interaction against this outcome.

There's an old trope about vets being hyper-sensitive when discussing their experiences. This seems to be a half-truth. Most—not all—servicemembers I know are tickled to share their tales, sparing no gory detail. I think Wally was different because he didn't want me to view him as a victim. He wanted to be treated like a fellow soldier. Not someone to be tiptoed around, because his story would have undoubtedly made our barracks hallowed ground—had I known.

Maybe this is why, after my fiancé bought the damn newspaper and we lodged ourselves in southbound traffic, I felt catharsis when she asked about Wally.

She tapped his picture. "You served with him?"

"No. Well, kind of. It's difficult to explain."

She took my hand. "Try starting at the beginning."

"It's a long and strange story."

Brake lights illuminated ahead of us.

"We've got time."

"Okay. Let's see . . . So, if you get hurt in the Army, the Warrior Transition Unit is where they send you to learn the high art of being a broke dick."

She laughed. "What's that mean?"

"Think of like a convalescent home for wounded soldiers. A place to heal in the presence of like-minded individuals."

"Sounds like an interesting place."

"Yeah. There's really nowhere else quite like it."

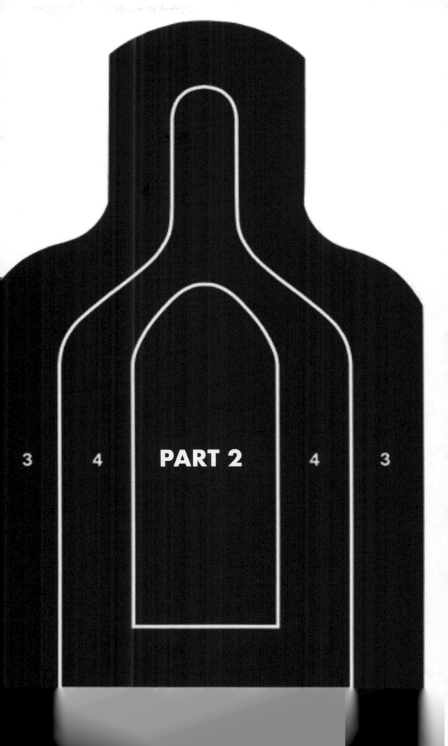

American Nesting Dolls

1. A Fobbit's Report

IN A HOOCH IN AFGHANISTAN, there lived a Fobbit. Not a swampy, bug-infested hooch dug into a rice paddy, nor a dreary lean-to hooch strung against a tree: this was a plywood B-hut hooch, and that means comfort.

All joking and Tolkien references aside, several years ago comfort in a warzone was my occupational specialty. Me, Guy Bradley, Air Force HVAC extraordinaire. While I call these writing's "A Fobbit's Report," a: as in a singular adventure, these writings are in fact a compendium of observations made during a six-month deployment to FOB Fleming. Not tales of audacity, badassery, and cunning, but tales nonetheless. In many cases I personally observed or was party to these accounts. Others I merely heard in passing and have taken great creative liberty to fill in the gaps. Continuity errors may be blamed on my status as an Air Force POG not privy to the slick, organic dialects spoken by the genus Army folk. My job was a singular experience, perhaps no different than any handyman operating in a closed environment in America (senior-living community, college campus, nudist colony). Only with our microcosm loomed the constant threat of death through indirect fire appearing as suddenly as rainclouds.

Of the many derogatory terms used to describe someone with an unsexy military job (Chairborne Ranger, POG, REMF, etc), I've affectionately taken to the term "Fobbit" because, well, I'm a fantasy-fiction nerd. Surprisingly, the many times I have proudly outed myself as said Fobbit have almost universally resulted in polite (if not sheepish) encouragement from combat-arms personnel. "Hey man, we all have a part to play here."

I hypothesize the main perpetrators of non-combat arms epithets are: (1) those constructing mythos to tempt youngsters into dangerous trades, (2) online fanboys, (3) traumatized units struggling to make sense of their lives after being re-subjected to the petty tyrannies of garrison life (I just saw my friend's face cleaved in two and you're grilling me about having my hands in my pockets?).

Being an airman on a predominantly Army-occupied FOB is akin to being a tourist in a foreign country; be polite when asking for directions, and most passersby will go out of their way to assist you. Work orders tasked me to nearly every tent or hooch spread across FOB Fleming, and in this way I was able to intermingle with a variety of military occupations. The following are their stories, such as they are.

Guy Bradley
SSgt, USAF
19 December 2015

2. Honor Among Slap Bettors

WHEN THE SLAP BETTING got out of hand, a platoon of New Jersey guardsmen made a desperate appeal to the aid station sergeant.

"Doc, we're betting over piddly crap of zero consequence. Slap betting needs to be sanctified."

Doc Brown pressed his fingertips together, tilted his head like the Godfather.

The other day Stewart and Alvarez bet over the candy contents of an MRE. Before that Defray and Hart literally bet over a pissing contest (Defray had no idea Hart was on creatine and chugging water like an aging model).

"Please. Please help us, Doc. We're one boring day away from dispensing with ROEs entirely. Mass slapping incidents will ensue, like a platoon of psychopaths."

The slap bet commissioner (an honorary title stolen from the same TV show that gifted them slap betting) was a vital check and balance. There could be no better man for the job than Doc Brown, a seasoned medic who was creed-bound to assist anyone who came to him. He humbly accepted, and under his guidance slap bets decreased eighty-five percent by the second week. Order was restored. Slaps regained purpose.

Then came a slap bet for the ages. The Super Bowl of slap betting. Could Wilson go an entire week without smoking? For his best friend, Tucker, Wilson's habit was disconcerting. Wilson would burn out his lungs before seeing twenty-five. Doc Brown hailed it a historic event: a weeklong slap bet. Immediately, side slap bets were brought to Doc Brown, guys pairing off on whether Wilson could or could not last. These were rightfully shot down, to not distract from the primary slap, so side bets were made with cash instead.

Doc Brown placed Wilson under twenty-four-hour scrutiny. A team of impartial observers followed him everywhere, even to the latrine, just in case he might try and sneak a quick puff. Regardless of the outcome, Tucker believed he had already won. He had used slap betting as a device to challenge his friend's smoking. If he had to take one to the face—so be it; Wilson's health was more important than a moment's pain and humiliation.

Wilson, edgy from quitting nicotine, saw things differently. That Seventh-day-Adventist prude had called him out, and he would have his revenge. Two days into it, observers spotted Wilson at the FOB's gym performing wrist curls. By the fourth night, they saw him meditating under a pine tree, tying a thin bandana around his forehead and rehearsing open-handed strikes under moonlight.

Tucker argued that the bet was about sacrifice. The military prizes heroic sacrifice above all else. Rather than jump on the grenade at Wilson's feet, he was jumping on the grenade that would explode in Wilson's future body. In his mind, they were not dissimilar.

On Slap Day, promotion flyers were scattered about the FOB, drawing spectators from several disparate units. Doc Brown wore blue examining gloves and checked Wilson's fingertips for tobacco stains, searched his person for loose cigarettes. Observers testified to his abstinence from smoking, and a shirtless Wilson emptied a bottle of water over his flexing right hand. The fight circle cheered when Tucker presented himself, opening for his entrance, closing as if devouring him.

Wilson toyed with his prey. His fat hand hovered over Tucker's smooth supple cheek, hovering and withdrawing—hovering and withdrawing.

"He's not going to do it," said a voice in the crowd. Indeed, some had speculated it would end in gimmick, a one-week buildup to a baby slap and brotherly hug.

"Pussy!" another voice yelled.

The crowd had not come for a tender Disney moment; they had come for blood. They had come to watch an eighteen-year-old private from Oregon get slapped in the face really fucking hard.

Wilson cocked a haymaker and swung at his friend. The crowd braced . . . and the slap melted to no more than a gentle pat, nudging Tucker's head sideways.

Tucker's face lit up as he opened for a hug, but Wilson gave a devilish grin.

"Psych," he said, slipping back once more.

The slap he unfurled should have delighted everyone. It was textbook, twisting his foot like a ballplayer hitting a home run. The smack was crisp and heard across the FOB. Gravel dust vacated Tucker's hair, who stumbled woozily but managed to avoid keeling over. It was exactly what the people had come to see, and it enraged everyone.

Instant division: no, no, no, the first slap was the real slap, the second slap was unsanctioned. The opposition: obviously the first slap was false and shouldn't count. The crowd was so torn over this debate, they began slap betting on its outcome.

"Order!" cried Doc Brown. "I demand order!"

Being the slap bet commissioner, the decision was Doc's and Doc's alone.

"I need a moment," he said, retreating to the aid station to think.

No one was stupid enough to do anything until his return. Wilson and Tucker eyed each other from opposite corners of the circle, remorse on both their faces.

Doc's ruling was that skin-on-skin contact constituted a slap. The second slap was out of bounds, and Tucker was now granted one free retaliatory slap. People cheered; Wilson blanched. Tucker was pure and innocent, but he was wiry as fuck. A former wrestler who could traverse the FOB walking on his hands.

They faced off.

"Double or nothing?" Wilson said. "I'll go another week without smoking."

Tucker asked if he really lasted the whole week without cigarettes.

"Of course," he said.

"Then I won't slap you."

Wilson winked. "But you didn't say anything about dip."

Doc Brown, the observer party, they all turned away, chortling. They had known. A whole week of chewing tobacco in lieu of cigarettes. They had known and technically it violated no rules. The slap bet was for smoking, not chewing.

Tucker screamed.

The last thing Wilson saw was a blurry palm and a flash of white light.

And they remained the best of friends long after the deployment had ended.

3. The Barber of COP Cobalt

I FIRST HEARD ABOUT THE CAV SCOUTS (Stetson-wearing cowboys) after a transient platoon of roughnecks swept through FOB Fleming's dining facility and filled their cargo pockets with all the soft drinks and potato chips we had. Within the span of one lunch period, DFAC shelves were rendered bare, like a post-disaster supermarket. The Cav Scouts didn't have access to such commodities on their combat outpost and were dependent on MREs and care packages for snacks. They also lacked a barber, and Cav Scouts visiting FOB Fleming were often subjected to appearance reprimands from ranking officers who didn't know any better (to which a common reply was to pantomime jerking off, leaving officers stunned and dismayed). Eventually, enough complaints were lodged against the Cav Scouts that their first sergeant, the only respected authority within their orbit, decided to take action. A local barber was hired on COP Cobalt.

Now the egghead who christened COP Cobalt must have had lapis lazuli in mind, that deep blue stone endemic to Afghanistan. But "Combat Outpost Lapis Lazuli" lacked the forward-charging or furtive edge most military names convey, so Combat Outpost Cobalt was likely a revised choice. Quite a few klicks away from FOB Fleming and adjacent to a bustling marketplace, an illusory veil draped overhead, contrasting the well-ordered military compound from the chaotic village at its gate. Troops stepping out on patrol swore it was like going from drab black-and-white to vibrant technicolour . Instantly: cherry red motorcycles beeped by vendors who passed out fresh-squeezed orange juice, and women hurried along beneath aqua-blue burkas, simultaneously seen and unseen by all.

Living so close to civilians, their first sergeant's grooming policy had been lax, allowing for modest facial hair in the hopes of garnering male respect. Now though, with FOB Fleming clamping down, the Cav Scouts were ordered "incognito as per the mission." Any trip to FOB Fleming meant they had to shave the night before, and an imminent visit from higher-ups forced them to ditch the ballcaps covering their heads and search for their dusty military-issued soft covers. Initially, troops loved the freedom to grow wild, shaggy hair that would be impossible to maintain Stateside. Oily tufts slicked behind ears like an SF operator featured in a *National Geographic* spread. But with First Sergeant's latest edict, they began to feel, little by little, the unbearable weight of an arbitrary system clamping down on them once more.

A barber has set up shop. Visit him. Pump American dollars into the Afghan economy. The age of sasquatch is over. Long live the age of pretty-boy GIs.

The barber was casually pensive, like a café Parisian with a master's degree in people-watching. He had a film star's gravity about him. An Afghan James Dean who survived beyond the tender age of twenty-three: soulful eyes, windswept hair. In hierarchical environments, where one's social capital consists of the number of pop-culture jokes tallied, his appearance was highly esteemed. And when troops saw Mr. Barber squatting comfortably on his calves outside his shop, biting a cigarette longer in ash than in paper, everyone agreed: "We have a Bollywood Tom Cruise working on our COP, and we don't know what to do with this information."

Troops felt invigorated by the charisma in this man's wistful eyes, which softened the annoyance of mandatory haircuts. Here was a man clearly destined for greatness. Unfortunately, the barber's looks and demeanor did not long conceal his subpar abilities as a barber, more an apprentice than master stylist. He buzzed the same military fade on every customer and specific requests were dictated to the air because he spoke zero English. Unlike the laundry tent worker, a beloved old man who would offer chai and enjoyed practicing his English, the barber, when approached by a customer, would extinguish his cigarette with wet fingertips before following inside, where a rusty hydraulic chair was the only context needed.

Troops exiting his shop examined themselves on polished surfaces, turning their heads this way and that. They examined each other, picking at cowlicks and laughing behind backs. The haircut wouldn't have been half bad were it not for an inexplicable final technique bestowed on all: a special set of silver shears were withdrawn from a leather holster and a perfect horizontal line snipped across the bangs, like a mother deciding on an impromptu bowl cut for her fifth grader. Troops nicknamed this bushy-mushroom shag "The Lloyd" and did whatever they could to mitigate it. Skip a shower and you'd be greasy enough to brush your hair up—evoking the barber's patented coif. Gel and pomade arrived in care packages, but the daily wear of a combat helmet always yielded the same messy results. The Cav Scouts puttered around the next month, dodging IEDs and kicking down doors on farmer-insurgents, yet most saved their fear and paranoia for the barber on the COP rather than the enemy outside the wire. This went on until one genius or maniacal PFC named Chance acquired a ten-piece barber kit, prompting a vicious haircut mutiny.

The haircuts Chance gave were infinitely worse than Cobalt's barber. Sides were left askew, the right more elevated than the left. He nicked ears and his hands shook like an FNG taking first contact. But a haircut from Chance and you managed to avoid The Lloyd. His technique for bangs—modeled off YouTube—brought hair up while scissors chomped across. On lazy days, troops would file outside the hooch for an appointment. Chance charged two dollars less than Cobalt's barber, and his skills were rapidly improving.

In response to losing almost all his clientele, Cobalt's real barber went from aloof to anxious. He was seen pacing outside his shop, smoking more relentlessly than ever, and he even learned a few English phrases to try and tempt customers inside. Eventually, he stopped showing up altogether. First Sergeant was furious at his boys for depriving a working man his livelihood. He came close to smashing Chance's clippers with a sledgehammer until he realized it was now their only means of haircuts. Second platoon was dispatched to recover the missing barber, but he was nowhere to be found. It was as if he had left the province. Left the country. Left the world. Then one misty Saturday morning, he returned, lugging a satchel of brand-new instruments as if nothing had happened. He opened his shop, turned on the light, and unfolded a rug for morning prayers.

A few passersby—intrigued by his reappearance—briefly considered a pity haircut but decided not to risk The Lloyd. It was First Sergeant's ethos of *lead by example*, that urged him inside. He had to see if all the fuss was justified. Maybe the barber's haircuts really were intolerable. For a touchy amateur boxer who buzzed his own scalp, this was his first professional haircut in many moons. And it was an utterly rejuvenating experience. Whatever technique the barber was going for with The Lloyd, he had mastered it now. Such swift and fluid *snip-snip* motions, the gentleness the barber wielded caused First Sergeant's head to swell with champagne bubbles. A massage was offered. Sideburns were boxed by the delicate scraping of a straight razor. First Sergeant left feeling decades younger, and troops mistook him for lower enlisted until they saw the ornate rank upon his chest.

"Damn, Top, you looking on-point!" one sergeant said.

It was true, too. The years of stress that had wreaked havoc across First Sergeant's drooping brow were now obscured by an intricate fringe parted to the left. Grown to excess and this look might resemble a surfer-dude or boyband haircut, but somehow the barber had fused youthful bounce with that of sharp-angled competence.

All it took was one promenade across the COP for everyone to notice First Sergeant and realize the barber of COP Cobalt was back, and this time he wasn't fucking around. Curious troops left Chance's line and—*yes!*—the results were consistent. They Skyped home to wives and girlfriends who gasped at their new do, biting their bottom lip and cursing fate that their men were 7,000 miles away.

Meanwhile, the barber's fame and renown grew to such an extent that word of his prowess reached us at FOB Fleming. Anyone who had the opportunity to visit COP Cobalt (not the most desirable of prospects) did so in pilgrimage to the barber. While the Cav Scouts still plundered our DFAC for sugary comestibles, we now came to them for haircuts. And it took one cut from a full-bird colonel for the powers that be to determine that "in the best interest of the barber," he would be better off serving on FOB Fleming where he would have access to a larger clientele and his fortunes would increase.

The Cav Scouts, so dismayed at the loss, said fuck-all to haircuts and became unkempt, dangerously unpredictable, and were generally better off avoided whenever they laid siege to FOB Fleming.

Us Fobbits enjoyed the barber's haircuts for many months until social media posts brought the barber worldwide recognition. Eventually, several organizations united, including a non-profit, a senator's daughter, and a B-list actor, and the barber and his family were granted visas to the States. This barber, you may or may not be aware, has since set up shop in Queens, NYC, where I'm told the wait time to see him is upwards of a month.

Of the many things I experienced during my deployment, truly one of the most memorable (and bizarre) is when we all looked fly as fuck in a warzone. And it's a crime and shame that no journalist or wartime photographer was embedded with our unit at this time.

4. Made with Love

PFC POULOS DRAGGED HIMSELF into the kitchen all mopey and depressed and stepped into his white apron, not bothering to tie it from behind. His attitude was a problem for Sergeant Hill.

"We serve soldiers dealing with Lord knows what," she said time and time again, "the least we can do is serve our food with love."

Hill wanted her DFAC to be a place where you could forget the war, if only for an afternoon. For some soldiers, a meal at her DFAC might be the only hot chow they got that day, or that week, heaven forbid.

A new grandmother in her late forties, everyone called her crazy for enlisting a year before her age would have barred her from service. In retrospect, joining the Army was one of the most rewarding experiences of her life—especially deploying.

And Poulos' bitter-betty attitude was wrecking this one.

Army life was hard at first, being stationed away from all her kids. Then Hill started adopting the children around her. A pseudo mother to all the young soldiers who trickled through her line each day, only a sneeze guard and a ladle of macaroni preventing her from issuing each of them a warm embrace. Poulos was one such adoptee when he first reported for duty. An energetic chef and amateur DJ, it's when they deployed to FOB Fleming that the troubles began. His parents were mad at him for abandoning the family restaurant in search of adventure, and he found the DFAC menus overly restrictive, he couldn't satisfy his artistic edge. These pangs were assuaged easy enough; Hill became his family, and they found small ways of sneaking in creative efforts: a little garnish for the key lime pies, extra ingredients offered to patrons at the omelet bar. But now he was lovesick, and there wasn't a damn thing she could do about that.

Until there was.

Every night after mopping up the DFAC, Poulos would log online and pine over Yasmine's profile. They were so close to being a couple, only to be torn apart by his controversial decision to enlist. He had thought the clean and green Class A uniform would impress her, even with his paltry three ribbons. For one magical evening it had, and he'd even gotten to second base. Now, as he studied her profile, he couldn't decide if he wanted to go home or stay in this warzone forever. Yasmine's latest post read:

You know your new boo is a keeper when he surprises you with flowers on a Monday. Falling more in love each day! Xoxo

Flowers on a Monday. Why hadn't he thought of that. He was about to slam his laptop shut when a message pinged.

Christy: "Hello there! I see you are friends with my auntie,

Sergeant Teresa Hill. She brags about you quite a lot, says you're one of the best soldiers she's ever had. I know she's your boss and all, but I wanted to thank you for taking such good care of her overseas. I hear you two have got each other's backs. By the way, I'm Christy. . ."

Who is this? She was beautiful. Studied social work at UNC. *Sergeant Hill, why didn't you tell me you had such an attractive niece.*

He sent a response—"Oh, it's no problem, she's a great section sergeant"—and then he asked about her. He couldn't break away, it's like they'd known each other for years. It was only the prospect of a 0400 wakeup call for morning prep that caused him to say goodnight. *Better this way*, he thought. He didn't want to come across as desperate.

The next night, he left the DFAC half-mopped and was elated to discover yet another message from Sergeant Hill's niece. Unable to chat live because she wasn't online, he penned a sincere note about himself: who he was, who he is, his hopes for the future, even his favorite football team (the Denver Broncos). He would do things right this time. Christy would not become another Yasmine. He always dreamed of someone special waiting for him Stateside, like all the cutesy homecoming videos where soldiers are tackled by eager loved ones. Could Christy be that person? Perhaps, if he played his cards right.

It had worked. After a few nights' conversation, Poulos had regained his puppy-dog spirit. Effort—love—was once more put into his cooking. He scooped full satisfying portions for each patron and smiled when asking "Veal or pork roast?"

And Hill thought she was terribly clever for orchestrating it all. That's more or less what she told her daughter during their weekly phone call.

"You know I'm not tech-savvy, so you'll be proud of me. I downloaded all of your cousin's photos—just the modest ones—and made a new account with a fake name and friended as many people as—"

"MOM. Oh my god—you're catfishing this poor boy."

"No, no, it's not like that—I swear. I have no intention of ever meeting up. I mean, how could I?"

Her daughter's reaction caused a tingly flushed feeling to spread throughout Hill. *Had she made a terrible mistake?* she wondered, especially after Poulos spent the better half of a dinner rush prying about Christy's favorite *this* and Christy's favorite *that*. And could she even keep up with all the messages he now sent?

"Catfishing is practically identity fraud, Mom."

"I just wanted to encourage him," Hill said. "I didn't think the boy would fall in love with me."

"Just what have you two been talking about?"

"Everything. Maybe I like it, too."

"Oh, Mom."

Something had to be done. Poulos was growing bold. Their chats flirtier and more personal. Truthfully, Hill would be fine keeping things like this, Poulos none the wiser. It changed her opinion of online dating, that's for sure. Age and rank had made connection such an insurmountable hurdle she learned to stop feeding desire. Surrounded by so much youth in the Army, it had been comforting to present herself as the wise "old person." Now she wondered if this persona had stunted her potential. Why couldn't she have had a fling or two when lower enlisted? Why couldn't she now? Her chats with Poulos were chipping away at a barrier of some kind, and that scared her. She couldn't keep stringing along this youth the same age as her daughter who had nothing but the world ahead of him.

She tried distancing herself: less frequent messaging, vague and disinterested replies, but she always found herself enticed by something he'd say. The idea of talking so openly with someone you care about was hard to let go; she'd learned more about Poulos as Christy than she ever could as Sergeant Hill.

She tried misinformation.

"What is it you like so much about Christy?" she said one day. "If you ask me—she's always been a problem child."

"Everything," said Poulos. "Her little jokes. Her philosophy that the best life is one spent in service to others. She's an amazing person."

Shoot, all that stuff is just plain old me, Hill thought sadly.

Poulos was released early that night while Hill stayed behind to mop up.

It was her daughter's idea, and Hill allowed it. Christy's relationship status was changed to *Engaged*, and the account was surrendered to Hill's daughter. Hill couldn't log on even if she'd wanted. It put Poulos in a funk. Sad and confused, a different state than his gloominess from before.

The minute the DFAC closed, he ambushed her.

"Why?" is all he said at first. "Why didn't you tell me she was with someone. Why didn't *she*?"

Hill claimed she never knew what the kiddos were up to these days and apologized for things not working out.

"It's just she made this place bearable," he said. "The endless hours, the sauna of a kitchen. It was like I had something to look forward to after each shift."

"I'm sorry," she said again.

"And I'm trapped on this FOB—this giant fucking campground—while life passes me by. I've got no one."

Hill pulled him into a hug. He offered passive resistance but gave in.

"It's okay," she said. "You've got me, Poulos. We've got each other's backs."

5. As Above

A CERTAIN CHINOOK PILOT who specialized in resupply drops liked to dazzle spectators with ballsy aerobatics. For the boys on a distant OP or firebase, having this pilot swing by was like being treated to a Blue Angels show, seeing this clunky helicopter suddenly maneuver with the grace of a small drone. Troops loved to watch the pilot J-turn a thirty-million-dollar piece of equipment, performing a reverse one-eighty as smoothly as a getaway driver in a heist movie. More than anything they liked the Jackknife, a momentary nosedive seeming to defy several principles of physics.

The identity of this pilot was known only to a select few, and troops on the FOB would often speculate about the maverick artist. Some even made long-standing slap bets should the pilot be revealed. Unfortunately, an incoming lieutenant, seeking to make a name for himself in the sport of unnecessary risk-taking, crashed a Black Hawk while emulating the Chinook pilot and was killed instantly. The deceased pilot was immediately replaced with a woman pilot, who statistically account for less accidents than men, and strict penalties were threatened for any pilot attempting flashy pirouettes.

In honor of the nameless and now suppressed Chinook pilot, several troops ordered remote controlled Chinook toys and began terrorizing FOB Fleming, performing the same tricks as their silent hero. Guards in towers reported Chinooks buzzing ominously outside like massive killer bees, and Afghan workers, who were also harassed, quickly retaliated by hurling rocks and knocking baby Chinooks out of the sky. So intricate and varied the Chinook games became, men lamented having to buy a new Chinook toy every other week after recklessly breaking their current model. The women, on the other hand, who engaged in the same antics as the men, somehow retained their original purchase throughout the entire deployment.

The identity of the mystery Chinook pilot was never released to the wider FOB community, though in certain Afghan villages the kids are known to race around with broken Chinook toys that will not fly but nonetheless serve as hand-held models. It's common in these villages for the children to tie kite strings around the toys and whirl them near their mothers cooking in the kitchen, mimicking noises that sound like "Swish-swish" or "Vroom-vroom."

Several years after the fact and before the Fall of Kabul, one village successfully churned out two helicopter pilots for the Afghan Army, one male and one historic female pilot. Neither of whom, throughout their sadly brief careers, ever crashed an aircraft.

Trigger Time

KYLE OVERTON FELT neither fear nor thrill when Selena told him she was pregnant with his child. No tears of joy at culminating a seven-year relationship with love incarnate; no sudden and claustrophobic urge to run for the hills and never be seen again. A pregnancy out of wedlock, the former sergeant mused, was the most military thing he'd done since leaving the service nearly a decade prior. Technically they were newly engaged, which made the miracle viewed as mishap slightly more tolerable in the eyes of his Catholic family.

His glory days in the Army had occupied his thoughts as of late. So much so, that during a surprise engagement party, he concluded that *a soldier can leave the Army, but the Army never leaves the soldier*. He'd heard similar aphorisms before without believing they applied to him. That old quote "A man fires a rifle, and his hands remember the rifle" seemed only half true, at least in a literal sense, when a civilian coworker named Rupert broke out a Colt AR between Ed Sheeran songs and asked him what he thought. Receiving the weapon in both hands, like an infant, Overton tried not to think of the business card scene in *American Psycho*.

"Impressive," he said, mentally chuckling. "Very nice."

He put stock to cheek, aimed at a bookshelf, and racked the charging handle half a dozen times.

"Could use some oil," he said more to himself than his coworker, but Rupert's head lowered as if he'd fallen short of an obvious expectation.

The weight and balance of the rifle felt more like déjà vu than muscle memory. He missed the feeding tray two or three times slapping in an empty mag. He could operate it— sure—but wasn't certain he could do so under pressure.

"I'm breaking this baby in next Saturday," said Rupert. "Care to join me?"

"Can't—I'm prepping a résumé PowerPoint for homeless vets."

"Show me how an infantryman zeros a rifle and you can use my slides."

"Okay. We can shoot," said Overton disinterested. "Sounds like a blast."

They shook on it and rejoined their partners on the patio. Overton's "blast" pun went sadly unrecognized. Interlacing hands with his fiancé, he felt the usual flow of oxytocin that accompanied physical contact with a loved one. That warm effervescent glow wasn't as potent as before. It could have been stress from planning a wedding plus baby. Or it could have been because as his hand massaged hers, his fingers twitched for the cold steel of Rupert's rifle.

The transition from combat soldier to college student left Overton prone to nightmares. Not the sweat-inducing flashbacks one might expect from someone with two deployments under his belt; no, these scenarios were more a commentary on his new direction than a nudge from his soul to process trauma. One such dream placed him in a close-quarter firefight where he couldn't for the life of him manage to pop off a round. He squeezed and squeezed a locked trigger before realizing his rifle was rubber and not metal alloy. In the dream world it made perfect sense the Army would fuck up and issue a dummy rifle. A classic "it is what it is" moment solved only by a shrug of acceptance before a flurry of enemy bullets forced him awake.

Easy Overton, his platoon had called him, because of his steady vibes. Always cool, even under pressure. He seldom amped up and never looked low. Overton simply was. A 20k ruck march traversing merciless Afghan mountains would elicit zero complaints, just as a three-day rest from missions would bring little change to his observant face. His stamina and fortitude served him well in Ranger School—where he lost twenty pounds, was recycled during Mountain Phase, but finished nonetheless. And while the coveted tab on his left shoulder earned him respect, many in his platoon called him quiet or stoic. Others saw him as "blank" or withdrawn, though this was far from the truth. Overton was simply one of those rare breeds of men blessed with unwavering emotional control.

Until he left the Army.

His famous inner strength, it turned out, came from faith in the military lifestyle. An odd comfort borne of trust and predictability. When Stateside, he knew where the motor pool was and when he needed to be there. He was on a first-name basis with a flirty hair stylist; and when sick or injured, receiving care was as easy as flashing his ID at the red-bricked medical facility. Even in war zones, most difficult decisions were someone else's responsibility. There were few uncertainties to stress over. Death anxiety was mitigated through comradery, and the choices he could make—what to have for lunch, where to vacation—offered just enough control to keep him satisfied.

The first pang of crisis for Easy Overton came two

weeks after discharge. Six years and two deployments had elapsed in which he was entirely dependent on Mommy-and-Daddy Army for his needs, and like anyone emerging from an insulated environment, the unknowns of the civilian world shook his sense of identity. Should he go to college, or should he get a job, and why hadn't he thought of this sooner? Why hadn't a therapist sat him down and demanded an exit strategy? *Prove to us you know how to care for yourself out there. Show us a school acceptance letter. Show us a job offer. Shit, just show us a decent résumé.*

Lacking both direction and purpose, those pesky human weaknesses quashed by military bearing burst forth, and Overton went from lean, mean, fighting machine to beer-bellied security guard at a data warehouse. Late at night, he patrolled waxed hallways and tried not to compare himself to the lapsed standards of the military. Long gone were the dignified days of service, but without accountability, without hierarchy, he refused to care. His job was easy and provided just enough income for rent plus Netflix. Then he met Selena, a woman whose mere presence made him painfully aware of his stagnation. Here she was, a jewelry designer with an LLC, and here he was—sitting on a ticket to a four-year degree while life passed him by.

Overton wasn't lazy; the logistics of civilian life were never fully explained to him. Almost like he was expecting paper orders sending him to college when the choice of what to become outside of service was his and his alone. Choice can be terrifying but also empowering. Each hammer stroke spent carving out a pursuit other than soldiering boosted his confidence and self-esteem. And as Selena often reminded: his many failures were not setbacks but vital steps toward success. He would study Criminal Justice—no, Business Administration, and after graduating Magna Cum Laude—he took a job at an employment agency as a Veteran's

Specialist, ready to go from apprentice to mentor, now providing aid to servicemembers who—like himself—might otherwise slip through the cracks, miss their potential, if not for the encouragement and unconditional belief of someone like Selena.

"Why didn't you write me off the minute we met?" he said after popping the question on a beach in Maui, his arm draped around her slender shoulder.

"You were a diamond in the rough," she said and nestled into him.

He would have called the line cliché but found her words endearing given her trade.

Meeting Rupert at *Sam's Shooting Sports*, a star-spangled gun range south on highway 2, Overton steeled himself against the "pops," "cracks," and "kablams," audible from the parking lot. The symphony of disparate calibers firing at random caused a strange mixture of excitement and unease. He avoided an official PTSD diagnosis because war was something he'd wanted. He'd voluntarily exposed himself to man's worst tendencies clustered under the guise of history. Behavior responses like PTSD are often caused by how people view an event and not by the event itself. And it was Overton's predetermined mindset—or genetic dumb luck— that allowed him to exit the Army psychologically unscathed.

Still, the staccato "pew-pews" caused him to blink as he crunched across the gravel parking lot to his coworker's lifted 4x4. Rupert swiveled out of his Jeep dressed head-to-toe in tactical haberdashery: tan boots, khaki cargo pants, and a navy-blue polo. Overton offered a nod and a handshake but made no mention of his friend's gaudy 5.11 gear.

"You nervous around gunfire?" Rupert said with a lop-sided grin.

"I guess it's been a while."

"No worries. Let's slap some targets."

"Do let's."

The rangemaster at the counter had kind blue eyes that could turn mean at the slightest mistake. He fingered a brown beard while Overton asked about ammo and range time, which came out to thirty dollars more than he'd wanted to spend. He swiped his USAA Visa and was sent with Rupert to lane 9. The gunfire heard from the parking lot was infinitely louder at the firing line, yet this relaxed Overton—being able to see where the noise was coming from.

They set their zeroing paper 25 meters out—the first thirty rounds or so devoted to sight adjustments.

"Would you do the honors?" Rupert asked, unzipping his AR (with a noticeable degree of ceremony) from a canvas case.

"Sure."

The rifle had been oiled. Rupert straightened his posture watching his colleague inspect the glossy ejection port. After making himself comfortable at the range's bench, Overton inserted a magazine, brought the bolt forward, inhaled, exhaled . . . and squeezed.

Blam!

Initially, Afghanistan felt less scary than Iraq. Instead of back alleys and colourful marketplaces there were charcoal mountains abutting clear, blue skies. With such open swaths of terrain, threats could be seen approaching from any direction, and moments of danger were surmounted by the confidence of those around him. For Overton, war was more fun than fright.

"A deployment's nothing but a year-long camping trip with your best buds," his platoon sergeant had said. "Only without the beer."

In fact, there was even beer. Or near-beer: non-alcoholic

cans that tasted real if drank for long enough. Overton and his pals would hoard cans and engage in spontaneous and increasingly arbitrary drinking games. If First Sergeant announced something via loudspeaker on a Tuesday, everyone had to down a beer. Anytime third platoon's CrossFit-bro LT was spotted in Ranger panties—no matter the day—everyone cracked a cold one. If the FOB was ever struck by rocket fire, Specialist Ross had to shotgun a beer. If mortar fire, everyone drank except Ross.

It wasn't all fun and games. Between running missions, pulling FOB security, and responding to local emergencies, downtime was used to rest, decompress, and not much else. One troop tried keeping a war journal but found himself binge-watching movies instead. Any hobby or activity even remotely taxing after a full day of gunslinging was quickly abandoned. The new guys earned Combat Infantryman Badges trading rounds with a poppy farmer. They suffered injuries and lost two friends during a complex ambush— now an infamous anniversary noted annually on social media. And returning home to process his second year abroad, the most alarming takeaway was the public's perception of American warfighters. His friends and family wondered if he was altered by his deployments. He wasn't. Not really. Blessedly. No more than can be expected after time served in a stressful occupation. But try telling that to a nation whose sole conception of war comes from popular entertainment. A nation that outsources its dirty work to 1% of the population, creating as much distance from state-sponsored violence as that of their sewage treatment systems. In theory, this stuff happens, but we'd rather not know about fine details unless it's packed into jarring headlines or pathos-evoking narratives.

Playing into tropes became a convenient and well-trodden social path for Overton to win sympathy and approval. This wasn't fake exactly and only required concentrating on memories that did startle him. Eventually, he told the same stories so many times to girls at parties that even he stopped trusting the gravelly and reluctant timbre to his voice. More anxiety came from belief that his 1000-yard stare was unconvincing than from memories of war, and it was only Selena to whom Overton could share his stories in their most nuanced and authentic versions—the depth of their connection encouraging a total understanding of each other. He could sit with a cup of coffee and confess how neutered and aimless he felt after leaving the Army and she wouldn't think any less of him. Just as she could explain her parent's disappointment after she chose to pursue jewelry design and not a sound field of study such as Medicine or Information Management.

Perhaps more challenging than the public's perception of the military was the military's perception of itself. As an infantryman, Overton was never forced to confront the honor taxonomy elevating combat arms above everyone else—he was already a member of the "cool club." More than that, after building enough trust with Selena, they both unconsciously decided the only person whose opinion mattered was each other's. A luxury, it seemed, not everyone possessed. When counseling vets at the employment center, time and time again, his clients would turn sheepish after learning Overton was Infantry with a Ranger Tab. Some would even thank him for his service —as if his sacrifices were greater than their own.

"I was just a cook," clients would say, qualifying their service as beneath Overton's.

I was just a diesel mechanic. I was just a linguist—an MOS distinct enough for its intellectual rigors.

"Just a supply specialist?" Overton would fire back incredulously before proceeding to validate his clients' credentials. "You signed a blank check to the US Government the same as me. I don't want to hear such defeatist language!"

For his downtrodden clients he often fabricated a parallel universe where non-combat-arms folk were heralded as clever for receiving the same pay and benefits at a fraction of the risk. Indeed, Overton joked that if he could do it all over again, he might have chosen a specialty other than Infantry—preferably something with skills valued by the civilian job market. He didn't regret choosing Infantry but some part of him was curious about other MOSs and tapping into these secret whims built easy rapport and deflated tension.

Oftentimes his role as an employment specialist was that of a life-coach. Encourage clients to chart a path where obstacles should be faced rather than avoided. Help clients break through self-imposed or social-imposed barriers. His heart wept for the homeless vets and vets with unflattering or punitive discharges: a bad conduct discharge or worse still—a dishonorable discharge. His job was to help these veterans and not to please himself by judging them. The same rambunctious energy that pushes recruits toward Infantry can also be used for mischief, and it wasn't hard for Overton to imagine falling victim to his worst impulses. If there exists a nexus between service and later social issues, it's difficult to pin the problem on any one aspect of the military lifestyle, particularly given the many positives one can take away (teamwork, attention to detail, discipline). Perhaps soldiers who later struggle were destined to suffer anyway, and the military acts only as a convenient scapegoat for a life predisposed to instability. Some speculate the military can turn troops into yes-men, excising one's ability to set boundaries and say "no." For this reason, Overton was grateful for his NCO experience, where he learned to lead and not just to follow.

Blam!
Blam!
Click.

"Mighty fine shooting," said Rupert, standing behind Overton's shoulder. "Let's say we make this more interesting?"

Overton switched from Fire to Safe and rested the rifle ejection port up.

"What'd you have in mind?"

Rupert fished a twenty out of his wallet and slapped it on the bench.

"Closest three shots to the bullseye wins?"

"Okay, but let's make it lunch instead of cash."

"Deal."

They Sharpied names on two fresh targets and sent the first one as far as possible. Shooting is a perishable skill and techniques had more than evolved since Overton's heyday. In fact, entire fundamentals had been rewritten. Instead of gripping near the magazine well for standup shooting, it was common to see shooters stretch their support arm in an exaggerated C-clamp, something Rupert mimicked from YouTube. What hadn't changed was the cathartic release of shooting. The rush of empowerment that comes through harnessing an explosion in the palm of your hands. An emotional transaction that—like any drug—carries a dosage tolerance. In Infantry, shooting was never boring but certain drills did become repetitive. And there comes a time where shooting non-reactive targets is as exciting as brushing your teeth.

Aligning front and rear sights, Overton remembered his military firefights. Most of them over before they began, a dump of adrenaline for only thirty seconds of danger. During moments of fight or flight, higher-order thinking is suspended and only responses built through training remain. Modern warfare is almost a bad joke: aiming and operating such delicate instruments with only large muscle groups functioning properly. The more time on the range and the more stress you endure before deployment, the more likely you'll react to combat as you should.

Overton fired three times in quick succession, his shots rote and lacking focus. Devoid of any element of danger, Rupert's contest felt trivial—like a constrained drive home after racing the Indy 500. Still, there was a nice grouping offset the bullseye. Not exactly Robin Hood, but Rupert already knew he would be buying lunch.

"Fuck me," he said.

"Guess I still got it," said Overton.

He set the rifle down and stroked it in jest. Petted it, like it was alive—something a human could bond with—and not a cold, inanimate murder machine.

Something primal broke loose after shooting with Rupert. A masculine energy long cornered and suppressed by polite society. Each morning a liquid-hot unease stirred at the base of Overton's spine, just above his genitals—a pang that could only be appeased by decisive action of some kind. The tension was inflamed by coffee but calmed by Selena's perfume. He began to crave solitude and discomfort. He rejected ornate meals in favor of bodybuilder-kibble: broccoli, chicken, and rice hastily cooked and shaken together in a massive Tupperware container.

"Are you training for a marathon?" Selena asked after noticing his morning runs stretch from thirty minutes to two hours.

In truth he didn't know what was happening. He hadn't been this gung-ho since his first deployment to Iraq. Back then, the unknowns of combat sent him scurrying to the gym each night, sent him drinking and partying with his unit whenever possible. Would he be a good soldier downrange? Could he trust his platoon? Would they perform well as a team?

It was like he was training for war all over again. A war that didn't exist. A hypothetical and hellish tour of duty where weakness would not be tolerated. Old neural pathways created by the military seemed to be activating in response to—what? Shooting with Rupert?

Without realizing it, Overton's trademark patience began to erode. His social values inverted. Things he was indifferent to now bothered him, and the things he once cared about he was now indifferent. Rupert was suddenly irritating. Rupert—with his paramilitary esthetic in choice of vehicle and wardrobe. Rupert—who owned an AR but had never carried a similar rifle into combat. Rupert—who if he wanted to walk and talk soldier should have joined the fucking military years ago—and should dispense with the playacting.

Even his clients' sob stories began to annoy. Each one of them arrived with a similar cocktail of stressors: unemployed for far too long, barely scraping by on VA disability, plagued by insecurities. Defeated. Depressed. Sitting across his desk with arms crossed and brows furrowed, forcing Overton to fake the positive regard that once came so naturally. The empathetic half of his ego who recognized himself in their suffering was fading away. Replaced by a disparaging monster who wanted to shake them by the shoulders and shout:

"Were you this fucking weak in Afghanistan? Where's your warrior spirit!"

But he never broke his workplace persona. He did his job, albeit with less enthusiasm, and saved his burgeoning aggression for other outlets: hours-long phone calls with military buddies, a solo camping trip "to think" that left Selena pregnant—irate—and home alone all weekend.

If anyone was victimized by Overton's new attitude, it was Selena. Instead of planning for *their* future, he seemed to be reminiscing about *his* past. Although his body rested on the couch beside her, his attention was directed at his phone. He would text his buddies things like: *Remember the dogs we befriended until LT shot 'em in the face?* Their back-and-forth messages always instigated a flurry of feel-good correspondence that would last hours, Selena a third wheel to a chat happening on his phone. *Remember when Ross went a whole firefight stuck in the porta-shitter? Ran out of TP was his excuse . . .*

His boys joked about a bachelor's party in Vegas but agreed Syria's civil war would be more fun. Get the squad back together and rally in an active warzone—one last hurrah before Overton's domestication. Selena dismissed these conversations as idle banter but grew concerned when he appeared even further disengaged from their present reality.

"Should we have the wedding before or after the baby?" she asked.

Overton shrugged. "Your choice."

"But what do you want?"

". . . Wedding after baby."

"Oh, okay."

". . . What's wrong?"

"I liked the idea of a baby bump in our wedding pictures."

His phone buzzed. It was a buddy calling to brag about a new motorcycle purchase.

"Whatsup gangsta," he said, taking the call and walking away. "Super Glide? I thought you were going for the Softail."

Now he's on a motorcycle kick, thought Selena, attracted to the idea but scared of being widowed before being married. She wished he'd hurry up with the phone call. If he wasn't in the mood to plan their wedding, they could at least discuss baby names. In the running were Rion, Remy, and Marshal for a boy, and Christina, Ava, and Maxine for a girl.

Each week brought a new gaggle of veterans to his office. The trickle never ceased. The work became as mechanical as shooting had once been. Build rapport, tweak their résumé, offer a pep talk, and spit them back into the wild. He felt himself slipping into another rut; the same malaise Selena inspired him out of all those years ago. Is this all there is? he questioned. Instead of searching for gainful employment in a similar field (education, business management, consulting), he sheepishly applied for private military jobs. Another stint in the Middle East would bring double (maybe triple) his current salary. It might bring him back to baseline; slate his sudden thirst for mayhem through steady doses of fear and boredom.

"How 'bout it?" he asked Selena. "One last ride before we settle down as parents."

"No," she said. "Absolutely not. You're literally asking to be absent the first year of our child's life. That's not worth any amount of money."

They weren't together when he was active duty, so he tried educating her on the military lifestyle. How soldiers are expected to miss major life events in service to their country.

"That's different," she replied.

"How?"

"Because you're not a soldier anymore."

He rotated his jaw left and right. "Look," he said. "I need this."

"But *we* need you." She clutched her abdomen. "Your baby needs you."

"C'mon," he said, laughing at her. "It won't even know I'm gone."

"It?" she said, her tone both incensed and dejected.

Immediately, he knew he'd done fucked up, but remorse couldn't shield him from the biggest fight of his life. He'd rather take on ten Taliban than Selena seeing red. She wasn't angry at the word—a simple placeholder pronoun; she was angry that after all this time, they still hadn't agreed on a name. Angry that Overton avoided discussing the matter. Angry he kept blowing her off, busying himself with bullshit. Angry she was planning a wedding solo. And if he wants to be left alone, he can spend the whole weekend alone, she more or less said before slamming the door and driving for her parents.

At that moment, the only balm for Overton was the vague inclination that if he said "fuck it" to responsibility, he might be able to die bravely in a firefight abroad, which would beat the slow, meandering death he was experiencing at home.

◎　◎　◎

A baby mama's not the end of the world, thought Overton. Not on a defense contractor's salary. Plenty left over for steak dinners twice a week. He'd be an active part of the kid's life

—obviously. Not that things with Selena had deteriorated to a hypothetical custody battle over an unborn child, these are just the simulations men run when drinking to cope with pain.

Selena's impromptu weekend away had stretched to seven days. Evidently, her parents could offer more stability than a fiancé obsessed with becoming a mercenary. Those days ballooned to months; several awkward weeks of Selena coming and going, residing mainly with her folks, growing brighter and rounder and more at peace. She couldn't plan for the wedding, but she had to plan for the pregnancy. Her girlfriends threw a gender-neutral baby shower, and her parents welcomed their eldest daughter home with excitement rather than concern.

Overton, on the other hand, channeled his angst into a strange hybrid of self-destructive-and-then-productive behaviors. He'd drink with Rupert till 0300, still peeved at his friend's paramilitary imitation but unsure of how else to vent. When not perched in a lawn chair sipping Bud Light, he was firing at the range, crunching at the gym—doing whatever he could to distract himself from the long-term consequences of his recent decisions. The excruciating ache he felt (akin to a full breakup) only pushed him harder. He clung to the idea of becoming a warrior once more, a goal-oriented way of processing his emotions. He thought he could rid himself of Selena by staying busy—by putting energy into action. Then they started texting.

Text messaging became their default communication because verbal calls would always end in argument. With texts they could think and strategize and avoid the inevitable fury of live conversations. Sometimes their correspondence would turn playful and affectionate, a joke or compliment spliced between rote notifications. Alone—Overton could do whatever he wanted. But alone was also lonely. He felt his mood stabilize whenever Selena texted something nice: a throwback photo or gentle reminder to pay the gas bill. Eventually, receiving any text was better than no text at all. Even the inflammatory missives written in ALL CAPS and accusing him of cowardice displaced the numbness of being alone. His phone buzzed—and his nervous system rejoiced.

"I miss her greatly," he admitted to Rupert after cracking and sipping his fourth beer. "She's massively responsible for making me what I am."

"And what are you?" asked Rupert.

He didn't answer. Just stared into the void of a nearby tree line.

"So, what are you going to do?" asked Rupert.

Return to her, was the obvious answer. Beg forgiveness. Discover meaning and value by embracing family life.

He awoke the next morning more conflicted than ever after receiving a job offer via email, sent from a private company but written in the stale language of government bureaucracy. Red lettering at the bottom declared that the message was Unclassified.

Sgt. Overton,
We are pleased to offer you a one-year contract with .....
to deploy ASAP to .....120 days on / 10 days off .....
This offer is valid for one month.

Suddenly, his thirst for love, which reached its zenith while intoxicated, was competing with his hunger for respect: for the honor that accompanies dangerous trades, for the adrenaline and dopamine thresholds accessible only under intense moments of duress. A perfect world would allow him to be both husband and warrior, but Selena was forcing him to choose. And how dare she? Didn't she understand how important this was? Didn't she see just how much he suffered in an office job? Which was the greater human imperative: love or self-respect? He wondered what his drunk self would choose and thought about calling Rupert for more bro-chair therapy.

The PDF contract was obscene in length and needed wet signatures on nearly every page. Printing and completing the document took all afternoon. Now came the fun part: scanning each sheet and returning it to the original sender. His phone buzzed halfway through the task, and he cursed his own chemistry at the thrill he felt. *Selena reaching out.* But no, it wasn't Selena. It was her father, texting in boomerish longhand:

> *Selena is in the hospital. She and your baby are at extreme risk. The doctors said there was something wrong with her amniotic fluid and are inducing labor. I just wanted to keep you apprised.*
>
> *~Frank*

Overton's training kicked into gear—a reflex at seeing the words *hospital, risk*, and *your baby* written in reference to *Selena*. He bolted for the door, leaving contract pages scattered like discarded newspapers. Countless traffic laws were broken en route to the hospital: operating a cellphone, a California stop, speeding (obviously), one red light, and an illegal U-turn.

The greeter at the hospital looked like the rule-following type and appeared nonplussed watching him race to her info desk.

"Your relation to the patient?" she asked.

"My wife," he blurted out and was directed toward the maternity ward.

Selena's mom stopped him at the door, a defensive stance—arm stretched out—redolent of a stiff-arm fend.

"If you go in there, you'll just stress her out," she said.

"It's okay," said the dad, standing beside her now. "I texted him."

The mom shot the dad a look.

"Kyle!" Selena screamed his name, and he pushed past them into the delivery room.

"He can stay," she said to the doctors who looked ready to throw punches.

The delivery wasn't what Overton imagined. After the doctors briefed them both on the particulars of their case, they had several hours to sit and stare at one another. Selena in extreme discomfort; Overton present but useless. It was awkward making small talk under such circumstances. *How has the jewelry business been? (Busy cause of the holidays.) You look fit. (Thanks, I've been working out.)* But it would be inappropriate to confront the things that mattered: the wedding? (yeah right). A baby name? (They could have done that, should have done that, but something blocked them). More than anything, how could Overton explain to the woman risking her life carrying his child that he was one email away from abandoning her in pursuit of adventure?

Hours later, the baby finally came. Naturally, painfully. Overton squirmed but watched every second. His son emerged into this world neither crying nor screaming nor breathing, it seemed. Not exactly limp but with arms dangling loose. The doctors took him and immediately began resuscitation on a nearby station, starting with an oxygen mask that engulfed his tiny face.

The new parents could do nothing but cry and hold each other tight.

Please God, please Allah, please whomever the fuck, *Overton bargained. If his son started breathing, he would* make it his life's mission to keep this family alive.

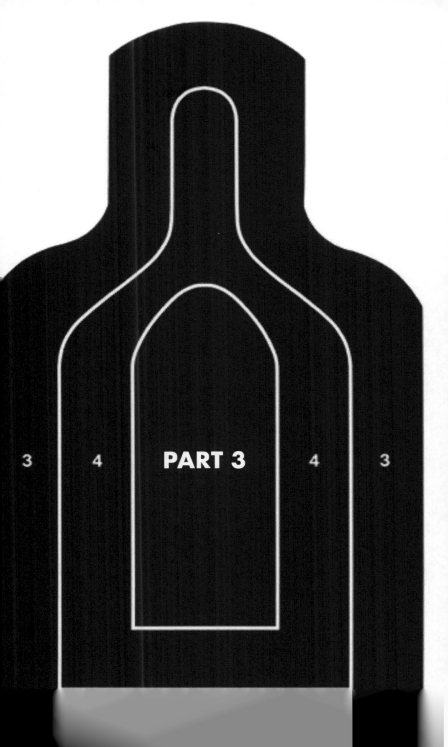

ON THE GROUND IN WASHINGTON

YEARS AFTER OP TIGER EYE, Grayson and I would meet at VFW Post 191 to discuss the particulars of our epoch. It was a safe place for us to kick back and comment on people's divorces and promotions. Comment on the mounting suicides we both felt powerless to prevent. Comment on each other. Without the rigors of military life, Grayson—whom I would learn to call Nick—had once again packed on the pounds, grown a beard, taken up philosophy, and started smoking a ton of pot. I was pretty much the same. Lacking purpose, maybe. Less dangerous by the day. Working hard to become an honest scholar.

One of our scheduled meetups happened to fall on December 7th, and Grayson—I mean Nick—had the fine idea of welcoming an Honor Flight of World War Two veterans inbound for Washington, D.C. Afterwards we would rendezvous at the 191 to brag about what decent people we were. I was less than enthusiastic about waking early for a traffic-intensive daytrip to the capitol, where we could—in fact—smoke pot but could not—in fact—carry firearms.

"C'mon, dude, we have to," Grayson said, sensing my

reluctance over the phone. "These people are our spiritual ancestors."

What we thought would be a tender gathering of interested citizens turned out to be a full-blown ceremony, covered by local news and emceed by someone who could have been inspiration for the Ron Burgundy character. Strong hair. A voice like drizzled honey. No mustache, though.

And then there were the veterans. They seemed taken back by the standing ovation they received on entry to the World War Two Memorial. One veteran fought from his wheelchair to his feet to salute a platoon of JROTC kids. If that didn't grip your insides then nothing would. They had lived full lives but were ancient and grizzled now. Relegated to serve their final days as "living history," as the emcee called them. As breathing monuments. A few wore their old uniforms. Although they were real, and I knew they were real, my mind couldn't break the association Hollywood had instilled by depicting similar uniforms that were mere props to a blockbuster movie. The uniforms I saw now were faded, the unit patches low resolution. A low-budget version of something I'd seen dozens of times before. But these were no verisimilitude—they were genuine artifacts.

The emcee began announcing the veterans by name, treating us to bios of their exploits abroad. A diverse spectrum of experience bound by a single denominator, *war*. A war, the emcee explained, that claimed 78 million lives; a war that re-tasked the auto industry into fighter-plane super factories; a war our country went "all in" on.

Introducing the veterans left to right, first up was an Infantry sergeant, Lord only knows how he was still alive (and standing, too!). There was a Seabee, an aircraft gunner, an intelligence officer, and down at the very end—past a few more men reduced to job titles—sat the lone woman of the group.

"Connie Morelli. An aviation machinist for WAVES," said the emcee.

"What the hell is WAVES?" I whispered to Grayson, who shrugged.

"The separate women's branch of the Naval Reserves," the emcee clarified before inviting applause.

"An aviation machinist? Oh—like Rosie the Riveter!" I said, rising, clapping, cheering.

And while Ms. Morelli was not exactly a Rosie, being a fully sworn servicemember, there was an iconic dignity about her. As if the trademark polka-dot bandana had morphed over time into a vibrant red scarf that coiled around her neck two times before tapering across her shoulder, the tail end dancing in the gentle breeze.

After the ceremony, the emcee encouraged us to descend from our seats and meet and greet the veterans. "Shake hands with living history, folks. The opportunity won't be there much longer."

We lined up, and it felt like taking something from them, shaking their hands. I wished it were more an even trade: some of my vigor for their wisdom and courage. Growing up, there had been an absence of elderly role models in my life, so to each one, I strangely wanted to say, "I wish you were my grandpa," but this would have unnerved them, probably, so instead I thanked them profusely for the freedoms they had earned us. We worked our way down to Connie Morelli whose weathered hand I cupped in both of mine—thinking it extra polite.

"Ma'am," I said. "Thank you so much for all that you've done for us."

She sat back and stared at me.

"Why?" was what she said.

"*Why?*" I said, alarmed.

"All I did was work on planes."

I think a slight wheezing sound escaped my mouth.

"Um. Yeah—yeah, but you had those planes going out faster than the Nazis could shoot 'em down," I said like an idiot, recycling a trite line from the emcee's speech about American ingenuity.

Grayson came from behind, pretty much said the same as me, but to him she acted like a sweetheart saint. Shaking firmly, smiling warmly, radiating that grandmotherly appreciation I seemed to crave. It was as if she sniffed me out as a compulsive overthinker and sought to mess with my day. And night. And weekend. And one more week of my life roughly one year later.

After a hasty escape from D.C., back to the poor-lighted comfort of the 191, I sipped my beer and asked Grayson, "Did I have an awkward exchange with that Rosie lady?"

He choked on his own draught. "Yeah, dude. Sounds like Ms. Morelli wanted to kill Nazis, too."

"Ms. Morelli," I repeated, which was probably better than calling her Rosie. "What a feisty grandma. But like come on, we just wanted to honor her. Some of us *need* this."

Grayson took a napkin to the froth on his beard. "What about when people thank you for your service?"

"I say—"

He had a point. For a time, I ran around snapping at people. "Thank your garbageman—I love what I do!" I would say to sincere, well-meaning people, never imagining what it was like on the receiving end.

Around our second beer, epistemic thoughts about truth

and perception broke through my sober inhibitions. Why had I never heard of WAVES before? When confronted by a World War Two servicewoman, the associated image my mind produced was Rosie, which wasn't quite accurate for Ms. Morelli. Rosie was a civilian riveter: she put . . . rivets into airplanes.

"Hey. Hey Niiick! How come they never made a movie about WAVES?"

He shrugged. "Hard to compete against D-Day, Dunkirk and Pearl Harbor. Heroes, death and mayhem—that's what makes blockbusters."

"We could do it," I said conspiratorially. "You studied film stuff. I could write that shit. We could base it around a young Ms. Morelli."

"Nah. They'd never let you get away with it."

"Why not?"

"They'd accuse you of being male. Inevitably, you'd focus too much detail on young Ms. Morelli's breasts and not enough on her biceps."

"Aww."

"Something like that would have to be written by Phoebe Waller-Bridge. Directed by Kathryn Bigelow. Maybe work in Clint Eastwood somewhere—I don't know, man."

"Yes, but I don't see where *I* fit into that equation."

Grayson directed his attention toward a modest flatscreen airing footage of the very ceremony we'd attended.

"There it is!" I shouted and pointed, beer mug in hand.

It was a landscape shot of the veterans at the World War Two Memorial. Next, an interviewer held a mic out to individuals.

"You know," Grayson said, "I don't think anyone knows what truly happened except those vets we saw today. When they die, the only stories most of us will know will be the ones Hollywood deigned to share with us."

"But how accurate is Hollywood?" I asked. "What do we lose by reducing war to a narrative form?"

"Everything's a narrative form. Besides, most war films are true stories. Or at the very least, inspired by real events."

I asked if he saw *Hacksaw Ridge.*

"Great fucking movie."

"The true story is crazier," I said. "At the end when he's being lowered in the stretcher—that's not what happened. In real life, dude gives up his stretcher to another guy more jacked-up than him, catches a sniper bullet to the forearm, splints his forearm, and low crawls his ass back to safety under enemy fire. All after he'd been blown up by that grenade."

"Holy shit."

"Yeah, Gibson skipped that part 'cause he thought it was too unbelievable for a film. So he just ends on Jesus symbolism. See, you can't get things one hundred percent accurate. Truth disrupts structural flow."

"When your war story is too unbelievable for a major movie—that's how you know you're a badass."

"Ain't that right."

Grayson studied the bubbles in his beer. "Hm. But would you know about Desmond Doss if not for Mel's movie?"

"Um. I would know of him."

"No, you wouldn't."

Before too long, Connie Morelli's name was at the bottom of the screen.

"There she is," I belted, spilling some beer.

INTERVIEWER
Ma'am, what do you say to the many
servicewomen in the audience who view
you as a trailblazer—as an inspiration?

CONNIE MORELLI

Oh, I guess we were trailblazers. Here
we were in WAVES invading this man's
world. And they put us through torture.
But once they saw that we meant
business—things calmed down after that.
It was the adventure of a lifetime. I
wouldn't give back a second of it.

Grayson and I had our mugs held high.

"Nor would I, Ms. Morelli," Grayson said for us both. "Nor would I."

ON A CLIFF IN MY HEART

A DECADE AFTER OP TIGER EYE, Nick Grayson would reach the apex of manhood by starting a family in the D.C. area. He had procured some sort of administrative role at VA Headquarters, a position he described as cushy-stressful, depending on the day.

Naturally, I would exploit his proximity to our great capitol, often showing up unannounced—like a stray cat—expecting a warm meal and a worn couch to crash on. He and his think-tank wife, Tracy, were more than obliging. I hadn't known such hospitality since Afghanistan. Never once did they deny me their basement as a Forward Operating Base in which to stage my D.C. adventures. So long as I could endure Tracy's indomitable itch to "set me up with someone," I could come and go as I pleased.

Family life suited Grayson, and his kids were a hoot. He was the man of the house. There was something so admirable about that.

He'd enter the kitchen and I'd say things like, "What's up, pops," before returning to the pancake breakfast Tracy had made for me and their precocious four-year-old, Jane.

One time, Tracy dropped a necklace down the sink, and

like reacting to contact, Grayson was down in a split second, twisting at the plumbing. Oily sludge and water splattered all over—but the necklace was saved. Tracy was so happy, even after I ruined the nice white towels trying to clean up after. They really needed him, his family. I've never known what it's like to be so necessary to someone, but I bet it feels good.

So, I always felt guilty coaxing Grayson out to a museum, a nightclub, or on a quick trip to Baltimore or Philly. Sometimes Tracy would be shoving him out the door, sympathetic to our need for male bonding. Still, here was a man with so much duty and purpose, he had no time for the spontaneous shenanigans I chased in desperate attempt to give my life meaning. Of course, Grayson cleared his busy schedule to welcome Sergeant Holloway on his retirement trip to D.C.

Holloway was to stay the week and leave before Christmas. Grayson's entire family would act as innkeeper and welcome committee, which made me a sort of tagalong uncle—less a special guest and more a reoccurring presence, like a neighbor's dog you sometimes watch.

I knew not to chew the furniture and to eat my food quiet and polite.

We had tracked Holloway's lengthy career on social media, watched him rise from staff sergeant to master sergeant, sending likes and hearts along the way. But a life filtered through select achievements is no real way to know someone. I realized this when Tracy, her kids and I, collected Holloway at Dulles International. Grayson had to work, and I was nervous-excited to greet our old sergeant. He was smaller than I remembered, though still very much the man who guided us on that mountain OP almost a lifetime ago. I spotted him at baggage claim, and we laughed endlessly because it seemed the most positive, natural channel for our many emotions. Our familiarity hadn't aged a day. There was a blurry-blank spot from who he was now to when I knew him before—for me too, I suspect—and our energy deferred to that point in time in which we knew each other best. We broke into a bear hug; even Tracy introduced herself with a hug. Before I could suggest otherwise, Holloway climbed into the back seat with little Jane and Grayson's snoozing one-year-old.

"Were you my dad's boss?" Jane asked, wide-eyed.

It was one of those random questions you'd never expect from a kid. Grayson and I had spent the last few dinners swapping our favorite Holloway stories, unaware Jane was following along.

With three neat fingers, Holloway shook her hand and said, "Actually, I like to think he was my boss. And you too, young lady. The American people—that's who I served."

Tracy eyed him in the rear-view mirror. "On this trip we're here to serve you, Sergeant Holloway," she said natural enough. "Wherever you want to go, whatever you want to see—just say the word."

"Ma'am—thank you kindly," he replied in the obliging tone of someone already decided. He then told us to knock it with the "sergeant" business. He was a "mister" now, plain and simple. A new title he'd earned as arduously as the former. We could even call him Calvin, he encouraged.

The freeway heading back to the city was surprisingly clear.

Grayson came home clutching two six-packs of Coors, and it was game on. Cheap beer you can drink quickly and copiously, a dormant superpower for most soldiers. Grown-ass men, Holloway an old-ass man, all retrograded to twenty-year-old warfighters set loose upon the barracks. Sadly, we couldn't get too crazy. Grayson broke contact to read a bedtime story to Jane, and Holloway and I did the dishes so Tracy could tend to the little one. Afterward, we four adults reconvened in the living room to reminisce about the Thanksgiving we spent at Holloway's, back when Grayson and I were still green and being hazed at every corner.

"You were so . . . innocent," Holloway said. He invited us on-the-spot after a surprise room inspection. Called and confirmed it with his now ex-wife.

"I remember opening your fridge and seeing eggnog. Just eggnog, no food. I was like what. the. fuck. These dudes clearly won't survive the long weekend, so I did what I had to."

"And after all these years, I finally get to return the favor," Grayson said, casting an arm around Tracy on the couch.

Holloway took a short pull from his beer. "Yes, indeed. I'm proud to say you've done well, Sir."

I wished in that moment I had established more a life for myself. I also wanted to impress Holloway. Look at me, Sergeant, I've grown up, too! But apart from vain intellectual advances, courtesy of the GI Bill, I was still the same boy who chased around a mountain cat all those years ago.

I couldn't decide if this should depress me or not.

Holloway woke at 0500, stuck in the basement with me and unsure of what to do with himself. "Please don't make me do PT," I said, bundled under blankets on an adjacent futon.

"Jet lag," he claimed, but I knew the truth. Twenty years of service had fixed his circadian clock to infantryman. He couldn't procrastinate even if he tried. Compared to Holloway, Grayson and I were tourists: our enlistment of four years and one deployment was like a summer vacation compared to his career of twenty years and five tours. Could we even call ourselves warriors?

"You wore the uniform," Holloway said. "End of story."

He didn't plan on being a lifer. Had half a dozen

ambitions back home.

"Every time I thought of leaving," he told us at breakfast, "I'd train up a new batch of soldiers—just like you two. I'd get to know them; I'd grow attached. Help 'em become better shooters, better leaders, better soldiers. In the end I could never let them deploy alone."

"So, the war kept you going?" Grayson asked.

"In a way."

"And now that it's over?"

He mused a second. "Garrison troops don't need leaders the way deployed soldiers do."

His more nuanced answer: after hitting the twelve-year mark, staying in made the most sense. Like the sunk cost fallacy, he'd already gone three-fifths to a full retirement. Maybe the same impulse that keeps us in wars, ironically.

I was about to broach the Fall of Kabul; twenty years of our nation's efforts—and Holloway's life—reverting to status quo. But it didn't seem like breakfast conversation. Watching internet clips of the Taliban strolling into their capitol was like seeing nature reclaim an abandoned shopping mall in a post-apocalyptic movie. Without committed groundskeepers holding the roots and foliage at bay, this was the inevitable outcome. Question was: would the Taliban tear it down completely, blow up the Cinnabon and break all the skateboards at Zumiez, or would they fuse it into something new?

Holloway's first D.C. mission was a wreath-laying ceremony at Arlington National Cemetery, something I'd heard about but never witnessed. He had "business" at Arlington, and the wreath ceremony was grateful happenstance. The molten-hot engine in my core activated at the thought of honoring our nation's dead. It may seem minor—laying evergreen wreaths on thousands of bone-white tombstones, but ceremony affects psychology in unseen ways. And what I thought would be a tender gathering of dedicated volunteers turned out to be a concert-sized crowd descending on D.C. Hundreds upon hundreds of people, all eager to remember the fallen. Who were they? Who on a cold December morning would wake at 0500 like Holloway and brave a D.C. commute to commune with the dead? Veterans! That's who. Or so it seemed. It's not like I conducted interviews but hang around your tribe long enough and you can sense them incognito. Heck, some were even active duty and in uniform. There were high-class veterans: strong jaws, aquiline, with clear, focused eyes and maybe receding hairlines. There were low-class veterans: a hodgepodge of super-rough people who stayed super-rough and others who used the military to refine their personalities. And let's not forget our beloved middle-class folk—people who didn't need the military so much as craved it. There were other classifications to impose if one wanted, race, gender, sexuality, but with all due respect, most veteran crowds consider these surface-level modifiers moot. We all bleed green, particularly on occasions such as this. Which is why my first philosophical conundrum was the absence of wreaths under Jewish and Muslim tombstones. The same whitewashed tombstone as every other but stamped with a five-pointed star or crescent moon in place of the majority cross.

"What the fuck!" I said. "Is everyone an Islamophobic anti-Semite? Why are they being skipped?"

"Jesus, dude," said Holloway, in reproachment or in joke, I couldn't tell.

Grayson smacked his forehead. "Wreaths are a Christmas tradition. *Christ-mass*."

"Oh."

It still didn't feel right to me. Looking down a line of tombstones: wreath, wreath, wreath, blank, wreath, wreath.

The point—as I saw it—was to honor the fallen. They were people of the book, after all, and we're all just interstellar energy trapped in a meat suit—what difference do cultural-religious inflections make? I wished I had a separate token to offer these bare tombstones. I thought about laying a wreath anyway but didn't want to offend anyone, so I bore these empty spaces like tiny pinpricks in my well-intended heart. Like a puzzle missing random pieces—so aggravating. This pet peeve was abandoned after finding who Holloway came to see. We had each placed half a dozen wreaths by this point, for this next one Holloway took the time to kneel and stretch out his hand.

Matthew T Clifton, the tombstone read. *PFC.*

"Nineteen years old," I said. My age when I deployed.

"He was the first one I lost," said Holloway, not looking at us. "Iraq, second deployment. I volun-*told* him to move from dismount to gunner. RPG shrapnel cut his carotid artery. You can't really staunch a throat wound that deep without choking the victim."

Grayson was beside him now, speaking too softly for me to hear. It's been said that a good leader is the reason you stay in a job and a poor leader the reason you quit. Here was one leader who flipped that equation: he stayed for his subordinates. And tortured himself for not being perfect.

I looked across the cemetery and saw hundreds of people scrambling all over. Most were cheerful—eager to participate in a little-known tradition. Most were laying wreaths and moving on. Others, like Holloway, were dropping to their knees for reasons unknown. I wondered how many similar stories were being remembered right now.

245,000 wreaths were placed, 245,000 wreaths would need collecting.

"Taking them down doesn't seem nearly as sexy," I said.

Placing the wreaths attracted quite a crowd. And God bless them. But a cleanup crew was just that—a cleanup crew. No larger meaning engendered by the task, and few would want to busy themselves with labor devoid of a larger context. This idea was only preamble to our larger fireplace conversation.

So, Afghanistan. Just what the fuck had it added up to?

Grayson broke out an eighty-dollar bottle of whiskey reserved for such a topic. So tasty, we sat sniffing and sipping for the first five minutes, rolling whiskey around our mouths until Holloway deigned to interrupt our palate cunnilingus.

We had all seen evacuation photos after the Fall of Kabul. Crowds frantic to be where we were now.

I pitied these people and wanted to help; simultaneously, a fresh start in a strange land sounded like the urgency I needed to make something of myself. I thought this but refrained from speaking it. I craved a fire under my ass. Starting low means it's still easy to climb higher—instead of levelling off somewhere pathetic as I felt I had done. But not everything is about me, and I was keen on advancing our current topic.

"Remember Khalid?" I asked, evoking the name of our old interpreter, unleashing a torrent of stories and memories.

Poor Khalid had endured more war than the three of us combined. For us the Taliban were an elusive enemy. For him they were a militant mafia. His family, who stayed behind when he came Stateside, would often receive direct messages: *we know who your son is, pay us now or else. . .*

"We should call him," said Holloway, taking out his phone.

"Drunk dial him?" I asked.

"Yeah. Fuck it. He's our boy."

His phone went straight to voicemail—which worried us some—but we left a boisterous message.

"To Khalid!" we cheered and took a shot.

Arriving in the U.S. on a Special Immigrant Visa, we wondered how well he'd assimilate. It pains me to say that with grim war bulletins featured daily in the news, acceptance and prejudice were genuine concerns of ours. "I am from Afghanistan," Khalid would say proudly to anyone who asked, and people would sort of tilt their heads at him.

"What's that like?" I remember one civilian asking.

"Not much different than here," Khalid said and winked at him.

Barely a week in the U.S., he was hit with a home invasion. Armed men in ski masks burst into his empty apartment. The only thing of value was a laptop his son was using to watch cartoons. The robbers didn't have the heart to take anything, but Khalid was rattled.

"America is very crazy," he said, almost suggesting things were safer in Afghanistan, which I know wasn't the case.

"To all our new Americans!" we cheered and took another shot. "May they have an easier time than those that came before them."

"He paid for my lunch," I said, recalling yet another story. "He was working at a clothing warehouse for minimum wage and took me to this Iranian deli because I said I missed Afghan cuisine. When the bill arrives, he snatches it from my hands. I was like—dude! You have a family to think of! I couldn't believe him."

Like refugees from the Vietnam War, we were confident Afghan refugees would make an indelible contribution to our nation because we'd already seen it firsthand. That alone was a positive outcome of war—pumping this country with cool people like Khalid. I don't think that answer would satisfy most, but honestly, it seemed to satisfy me. And we agreed: fighting in war was one of the coolest experiences of our lives. The trouble was—I was stuck in the past, clinging to the glory days of my naive youth. War gave me a range of emotions and experiences I couldn't have received anywhere else. Everything felt trivial by comparison. Oliver Wendell Holmes said that a man's mind, once stretched by a new idea, never regains its original dimensions. War had stretched my soul to an infinite capacity, and I struggled to fill the cosmic void within me. Grayson filled it with family; Holloway with his impressive career. Strangely, more war might do it for me, too. How envious I felt reading about top-tier vets sneaking around Kabul during the evacuation—getting our people out while writing a blockbuster screenplay along the way. Is this ache—this impulse—why war never ends? Am I the problem?

A more responsible thing to do with my longing might be to bear witness. Not saying veterans are magical, in fact we can be whiney bitches at times, but maybe society needs us to provide a sort of spiritual homeostasis. Win the war, lose the war—the war is just a metaphor for something grander happening inward. Something we must all confront. Cancer is horrid but spend an hour in a cancer ward and I dare you not to be affected. You'll leave with a perspective and balance as necessary to the human psyche as Earth's axial tilt is in relation to the sun. Without such awareness, you'll burn or freeze to death.

I'd fallen into a meditative trance. Coming out of it, Grayson and Holloway had skipped ahead and were discussing gang violence.

"I'm just saying," said Holloway, "All those key leader engagement missions to counter the insurgency—apply that same strategy to the hood."

"I can get on board with that," said Grayson.

"Picture it: a platoon rolls up in minivans instead of MRAPs, armed with love and respect—shaking hands with community pastors and gangbangers alike. It's high time we win some hearts and minds in our own damn country."

Several days later, we dropped Holloway off at the airport. Tracy, the kids, everyone came to bid him farewell. We had made so many new memories during his short visit to D.C., I didn't want to say goodbye. Grayson had a fitting response:

"When I think back on my life, memories abroad and memories of friends stand out the most. Brief windows of novelty that break up the monotony of day-to-day."

We were standing in a little prayer huddle, and Holloway went next.

"Life is a summation of the stories we tell," he said. "And the stories we tell about war can reveal the most."

These two veteran storytellers had made a mountain in a warzone as fun as summer camp. I'll always love them for that.

"War is a tricky business," I said, trying to match their eloquence. "Full of the highest highs and the lowest lows. But without it—I wouldn't have met you fuckers!"

"True," said Holloway, "We'll always have Afghanistan."

In that moment I felt like snapping to parade rest one last time. *O Sergeant! My Sergeant!*, I imagined saying. Grayson would have probably followed suit. A sorry sight to behold: us emotional old warfighters weeping at the airport. Instead, we let Holloway go unencumbered. Off to stand in the security line, luggage at his feet. He knew, as well as I, we would see each other again.

HONEYCOMBS

MY WIFE PRINTED OUT ARTICLES from Veterans Affairs on therapeutic journaling and gifted me with a smooth Moleskine notebook. I would have been fine with wirebound. She says my memories are too important to be written in something costing $2.29 at Staples. She still believes in ceremony.

Most days I get no further than rubbing the smooth Moleskine shell for luck. It seems to activate a calming nervous system response in the same way petting my dog or handling my stacks of Canadian Gold Maples does. You pay attention to these sensory things when you have an dysregulated nervous system. That way you get a clue on what your automated responses might be to external stimuli. That way you can head things off before they overwhelm you.

So, I get bullied into opening this thing, and I thought I'd build a chronology, then I thought I'd write ideas as they came, then I thought I'd build a chronology after writing ideas. "Don't overthink it," my wife says. I don't think I would if this was wirebound. My family didn't have a lot of disposable income as a kid, so the monetary value of this thought-repository sets the bar pretty high. I don't want to fill it with junk.

The first thing I should focus on is my present condition. I am not well. Like Dostoyevsky's famous opener in *Notes from Underground*, I think there's something wrong with my liver, *ha ha ha!* In truth, having kicked booze very recently my liver has never been better. It's my mental or emotional state in need of repair.

I suffered an IED same as everyone. Mine was a grouping of three, spread across two deployments. It wasn't one big one that took me out of the fight, just a series of concussive blasts resulting in sprains, concussions, and stress fractures. Nothing pierced me, even when a dismounted IED knocked me on my ass. Despite this, I can't help feeling there's a huge red chunk missing from my core.

The most annoying thing about it all: I don't know if this is curable trauma, or is this just the way I am now?

Booze was easy to beat. Easier than for most, I guess. My addiction was one of habit. I've seen guys emotionally dependent, and I've seen physically dependent. Try to stop when you're in the emotionally dependent stage. Here, if you solve enough personal problems you beat the booze by byproduct. (This I'm uncertain). Physically dependent is a much different beast. Maybe this is why they call destructive behavior a spiral. You feel bad so you take substances, and now your body needs them. Your body needs them so you take substances, and now you feel bad.

It took a while to awake to the fact booze was holding me back (rhyme unintentional). Typically it goes like this:

7 pm rolls around, and I feel I've done all I can to be productive that day (yet still possessing a surplus of energy), so I crack a beer. Then another. And a shot of bourbon before bedtime. 3 drinks a night ain't bad; plenty of guys do worse

to themselves. It was one of those wounded warrior surveys that had me math this out. The research studies where they pose the same question fifty times for a $20 Amazon gift card.

> During a day I have. . .
> *A. 0-3 drinks*
> *B. 3-10 drinks*
> *C. 10 + drinks*

I select *A*. Next question.

> During a week I have. . .
> *A. 0-10 drinks*
> *B. 10-25 drinks*
> *C. 30 + drinks*

I select *B*. Next question.

> During a month I have. . .
> *A. 0-20 drinks*
> *B. 20-50 drinks*
> *C. 50 + drinks*

I select *C*. . . Holy shit. Try admitting that on a job application. So, I start cracking a variety of nasty-ass non-alcoholic beer interspersed with cans of kombucha and La Croix. If my brother can kick heroin with pot, then I can kick booze with bubbly beverages. It seems to satisfy the 7 pm itch. Though now everyone makes fun of me for drinking "piss water." (Jokes on them—I might just live to see fifty).

According to the Army, I showed no sign of traumatic brain injury. I believed this for years and was never dissatisfied. This diagnosis was back when I was newly discharged and ready to trade my blood-stained ACUs for a navy-blue fed suit, or cop uniform, or even firefighter overalls. Back when I believed I would become something else. *My length of service will not be the defining characteristic of my life*, I thought. After a decade spent failing to achieve any of my ambitions, I started to suspect there might be something wrong with me after all. I needed something to blame. My sleep schedule was out of synch, and I couldn't concentrate on menial tasks because of what felt like baby ants marching circles behind my eyes. Once again, we come to a causality dilemma (a spiral): did the ants cause the insomnia, or the insomnia the ants? This was also around the time my poor wife learned about the honeycombs.

At first, she didn't want to share it with me, an article published by a major university describing secret brain damage found in IED survivors. Researchers performed autopsies—cut open brains—on vets who died of other causes years after withstanding a blast. They describe it as "honeycomb patterns of broken and swollen nerve endings found throughout vital regions of the brain, including those responsible for decision-making and executive function." A more journalistic piece citing the article speculates that these honeycomb patterns are the true culprit to the social and emotional problems plaguing veterans. The language was hedged: "might play a role; should be looked into further," but the implication was clear: if you encountered an IED— let alone three—you might be marked for life.

"You're right," I tell her after setting the articles down. "You shouldn't have shown me this."

I'm constantly worried about cause-and-effect narratives becoming self-fulfilling prophecies. How many PTSD tropes does a vet need to see on TV before they start thinking they are affected with the same maladies as their favorite hard-drinking hero? So, right now, I can't stop thinking about the honeycombs. It's the perfect excuse I need for failing to achieve my own high standards of success. It's an insidious and unconfirmed aspect of my story I'd rather not know about.

Here's another aspect of my story I'd rather not know about: In OEF we convoy to a faraway village for outreach and discover a boy who had been shot three times below the belly button by Taliban. He's lived like this for months, somehow, swapping bandages multiple times a day to stem the shit these intestine wounds secrete. My God. We get this kid back to the aid station and treat him properly: new bandages, antibiotics, a surgery planned at a major FOB. Big heroes, right?

Wrong. That's when Doc pulls me aside. "There's something you should know," he says. Turns out the boy's wounds are not consistent with the 7.62 rounds favored by the Taliban. If Doc had to guess, he'd say something smaller caused this. Smaller, like the 5.56 we all carried in our M4s. Of this he is uncertain.

For the longest time, I prefer the version where we're the big heroes. A decade later I come to believe the only way to properly engage with life is to speak the truth in its messy entirety.

Being sound of mind—I've come to believe—is a matter of balancing your nervous system, which in turn impacts your emotional state. To that end, I have a number of daily quirks that chip away at my confidence and create anxiety. It's like my nervous system is too sensitive, "flinchy," as I call it, in need of recalibration.

Returning home, I couldn't maintain a proper following distance on the freeway. Everything felt too close. Like in a split second, I'd slam into the car ahead of me and we'd both explode on impact. I still have car phobias. A constant weight hanging inside of me. I just know my ten-year-old hooptie in need of a new clutch will stall on the freeway and instantly cause a pileup—which then explodes. The ice-cold pop rocks crackling under my skin whenever a car merges next to me is an involuntary response to which I wish had an "off" switch. I've learned these banal fight-or-flight ticks are best balanced by physical release. Very inopportune for daily life. I can just imagine landing a desk job—battling hair-raising traffic—and arriving at work with the pent-up need to beat the stuffing out of a heavy bag before I can concentrate on morning emails. Because of this, I often engage in high-risk activity, which seems counterintuitive. Apparently, my adrenal glands need expressing just like my dog's anal glands. You go too long without doing this and a foul discomfort builds within. Skateboarding has become as Zen for me as meditation for a monk. And you wouldn't think riding a motorcycle would help, but on a bike, I feel none of the limitations I do crammed in a car.

So, one day I come limping to the fridge for an icepack, and my wife suggests I discontinue skateboarding. "It's taking too great a toll on your body," she says. She's right and indoor rock climbing would be a suitable replacement if not for the exorbitant membership fees. Growing up poor isn't a social condition, it's a lifestyle. Even if you break free of it, you're never free of it. I could win the lottery and I'd still recoil at the thought of 130 bucks a month on "self-care."

I wonder if the VA has any rock-climbing programs? If I had a choice between rock climbing or the benzos they prescribe, I'd take the rock climbing.

The next time the boy with the bullet wounds visits our aid station, our terp relays the full story. The boy got caught in a firefight while working in his father's fields. Bullets flying from two directions, an inescapable bubble of death. When the shooting ceased, both sides went their way, and the boy was left in the dirt to bleed out. No one can fathom how he survived. Naturally, he becomes our miracle child of redemption, born in a Far East village. We're hellbent on saving him, and the more active and violent missions get put on hold until we can make this kid's life better. His surgery is set. We get money and supplies for his village. The docs are scrubbed and ready to go, but the kid is a no-show. We drive out to his village. Everyone ignores us. "What kid?" one guy says to our terp. We knock on doors, but it's like he never existed. Some mirage dreamt up by us who want to help more than harm.

Later, word reaches us through backchannels that the Taliban threatened the lives of his entire village for cooperating with U.S. troops. What happened to the boy after that, nobody knows.

My wife prints off more articles and sticks them to the fridge on her way out the door. She goes to her legal internship and leaves me with the dog to ponder the weird, esoteric, new-agey gobbledygook she found online in a desperate attempt to cure me. This one is on sacred geometry. Some dude named Thomas Browne claimed the "Quincunx" was mystical evidence for the wisdom of God. The Quincunx (five dots on dice) is an oddly pleasant pattern found throughout nature, including the shape of honeycombs. I can't confirm I have a honeycombed brain without cutting it open, but her articles are a fascinating reframe. It would be nice to think of myself as a mystic and not a moron. Kinda like my man Dostoyevsky, who labeled the harsh epileptic seizures he experienced as a blissful tension within his mind, possibly the source of his literary genius.

What concerns me most is my wife's concern. I'm worried she's worried about me. I don't want her to feel bad for telling me about the honeycombs. For creating another spiral.

I'm struggling. She sees me struggling and tries to help. Her help makes it worse. She sees that her help makes it worse and feels bad. I see she feels bad for making it worse, and now I feel bad for making her feel bad for trying to help.

And round and round we go.

Rambo First Blood is on TV. Neither of us have seen it, so we nuke a bag of popcorn and cozy on the couch. The credits hit me like 7.62 straight to the plate carrier. Jesus. I thought I was watching an action hero movie. Did anyone in 1981 movie theatres expect Stallone's performance at the end? I know I didn't. I feel so bad for the guy, which translates into emotional resonance with all Vietnam vets. I have to remind myself it's just a movie. To what extent vets grapple with stuff like this in real life, I'm uncertain.

It's not just Rambo. Lately, I find myself emotionally affected by every war film. I can't even watch the trailer to *Hacksaw Ridge* without bursting into tears. It makes me wonder: how did the tough-guy conception of Rambo come into being? From the sequels, I guess. A roided-out impossible-to-kill superhero must have been a bigger hit with audiences than the broken man crying at the end of the first one.

Here's my experience with Rambo types.

They were everything I wanted to be. I was jealous of them—and I still am. While we got sent out to the middle of nowhere with a "shoot me" sign on our backs, they got ushered in for surgical strikes. They got to Skype with their girlfriends back home; we got to watch our ANA partners shit dysentery.

One mission, it's o-dark-thirty when we set security for Rangers outside this village we're trying to befriend. They come stealthing up to this compound, blow the doors off with C4, shoot a bunch of people, take a bunch of people. Their EXFIL arrives and "poof," they're gone. The village wakes up at first light and discovers some of their neighbors are missing and dead. They're mad as fuck and forming a crowd. We try to explain that elite soldiers had to take their neighbors, but they don't know the Rangers, they only know us. They're getting more volatile. Last week we were here with Army engineers trying to dig a well, and now it's looking like we're gonna have to mow down this entire fucking village just to make it out alive, a do-not-pass-go straight to Leavenworth. This is transpiring and all I could think is if I were just a little bit stronger or taller or smarter or better bred, I might have gone to Ranger Indoctrination Program and been with those fuckers who caused all this and then ghosted. I might have lived my highest ambition as a soldier instead of pissing off a bunch of third-world farmers who want nothing now but to kill us non-stop.

That's what I know about Rambo types, and I still wish I was one of them.

Things got pretty dicey for us after that.

My wife gets frustrated when she wakes to find me snoozing on the couch and not our bed. Nothing I say satisfies her insecurities. I tell her it's too hot in the bedroom (blame it on something neutral). When that doesn't work, I blame myself. The only thing worse is having her believe she is the problem and then having to go about my day knowing I caused her pain.

I've tried all manner of ancient potions and modern fixes to rid myself of insomnia. Melatonin, meditation, exercise, (valerian root was a fun excursion). Turns out, all I needed was to be digesting something heavy and sweet before bedtime. Protein shakes work well, but a glass of whole milk with a few squirts of organic honey is better. Don't ask what desperate midnight state I was in—thumbing through an old King James—to experiment with that therapy.

Discovering this was a big win for me. I think: if I can unearth enough fairy-tale solutions to my problems, and if I solve enough of them, I might just be okay. I might go on to become something. It's not perfect. I still find myself with racing thoughts at 0300, prompting me to tiptoe to the kitchen for a second helping of milk with honey.

Sometimes my wife still finds me on the couch.

I'm worried if this honeycomb thing goes mainstream, many vets will think they have a ruined brain and sink into a constant state of doubt (like me), unable to confirm or deny if they do indeed have the motherfucking honeycombs. Would this revelation flood the VA rating system?

"I got blown up, and now I got the honeycombs. Gimme money."

Could I get a higher VA rating?

No, a higher VA rating would sink me. What I need is a job with half the purpose I experienced in uniform. I deployed under fraught conditions. Counterinsurgency does not work; we know that now. If you're going to engage in a culture battle, you might as well do it behind a debate podium—aiming a microphone at your opponent and not a rifle. Even so, there's no denying us boots-on-ground folk had the best of intentions. Our missions sent to help people were undeniably meaningful. Instant dopamine affirming your identity as a badass do-gooder. In that regard, I have to thank the Army for letting me be a good soldier. The one time in my life I was good at something and of use to someone.

Sometimes I read these entries and wanna smack the shit out of the whiney sap who wrote them. I hate that I've become such a sensitive, frail, self-loathing twat.

How have we arrived at divorce?

Writing this question makes it feel so sudden. Like my higher order brain is only now registering a decision made by my primordial mind. The truth is, we've been unhappy for some time now, and we've finally decided to pull the trigger. I'm not fit to be a husband. She pulls an inordinate amount of weight, and I know it stresses her out. We've been more roommates than lovers for far too long, and it's time we release each other from unfulfilled obligations. Besides, we're ill-matched. She needs someone on her level. Her ability to navigate the social complexities of mainstream America is so foreign to me it's practically a superpower. Introducing the latest Avenger: High Performance Woman. She'll ace any interview, succeed at any job. Her network is vast and her record as clean as her teeth. Did we mention she speaks Spanish? She has direction and purpose whereas I'm lost in a sea of ambiguity, left to create meaning from discarded dreams. In the military, there was always a clear objective, at least at my level. Even if the task was impossible, you had no choice—and pitting yourself against any challenge felt like moving forward. The civilian world is too chaotic: I could pursue this; I could become that. I could waste ten years in retail, too nervous and risk-averse to map out something better.

Most days I want to start all over. Go back to eighteen with the knowledge I have now. It feels like I've glitched this world. Killed a vital NPC in an Elder Scrolls videogame and can no longer complete the main quest. Destined to forever roam this limited world where only petty achievements can be won. (Is this how ex-cons feel?) I just want to go back. Back to when I had limitless potential and only lacked guidance.

The last time I felt some semblance of value was on a QRF mission.

This ANA truck gets hit. They're gone. There's a fender over yonder and the rest looks like the early stages of a car getting crushed into a cube. (The fact they were riding Ford Rangers is an absolute dereliction to the value of human life, but I digress). We show up and trace wire fragments to a det site and follow footprints—no joke—to a group of shady characters reveling by a river. They're rocking old-school BDU pants, and we almost mistake them for ANA until they start shooting at us. We kick into gear: battle drill 1-alpha, baby! Suppressive fire, flank left, lob a couple 40mm grenades; they picked a fight with the wrong fucking platoon. It was such a quick turnaround from fear of death to group success, we didn't know how to come down. We had snorted pure energy and only wanted more. Energy meant for survival was now let loose in triumph. LT was calculating how to write this in a report, and we're practically humping each other in a group hug of shared invincibility. Give us another ten firefights like that, just show us where they are.

Experiences like this alter your DNA. Then you get back to the world and find out none of it mattered, on any level whatsoever. Shut up and go to college. Pick a number—back of the line—and compete for a soul-crushing career at Amazon. By the end, you're just so fucking tired, and the last thing you want to do is climb another hierarchy. Most vets attempt this, though. In the same way you get on a fairground roller coaster stuck to a fixed track. For them it's high and exciting; for you, it's a small hill. And it's like you're the only one who can see it's only going one direction, so while everyone else is screaming with their hands in the air, you're sitting there bored and questioning your decision to buy a ticket in the first place.

Everyone keeps advancing: getting married, earning new degrees, having babies. The best I can do is fight against my many foibles.

Stephan was just promoted to Chief Executive Officer of Consumer Relations, woman at house party says, martini glass in hand. Now we make six figures.

That's great! I say, NA beer in hand. I just went a whole month without watching porn.

I'm like the Benjamin Button of responsibility and purpose. While everyone else keeps ascending social strata, I keep spiraling backwards, all alone. I was married and convinced I'd become something. Now I rent a room in a houseshare found online.

Secretly, I pray for another 9/11.

I'm losing my ability to make simple decisions for myself. A cashier at the grocery store asks if I want to sign-up for their rewards program and I freeze. I don't know—do I? There's just too much noise to process these days.

Two plainclothes cops stand behind me at the checkout counter—they place a single carton of coffee creamer on the belt. Probation their tan polos read, slick firearms at the hip. While they appear alpha-like, their faces are so bright and unadulterated, like they've never known a bother in the world other than the constant annoyance of maintaining authority. "I wish I had your job," I say to them. They sorta shrug. I learned after discharge, the more complex your history is the more unlikely you are to get hired in law enforcement. They'll send your sorry ass to get blown up by Taliban, but no fucking way are you allowed to improve your community back home. They need girl scouts and altar boys for that. Hotshots who haven't yet been broken down. Younglings who still think they're God's gift to civil service. People who haven't yet learned how simultaneously resilient and vulnerable the human body really is.

Yes, I'm jealous. Jealous these dudes probably grew up with people in their lives telling them not to drink too much, not to fight too much, not to fuck too much. Jealous of the stability and purpose they take for granted. If I could assume an identity like theirs, I'm convinced all my worries would dissipate. I never thought I'd be anxious like this after leaving the service. And I know now that my service did not do this to me. America did this to me. The pressure and demands of modern life collect inside you like deadwood—and my service is the spark. Ordinarily, a spark is bright and warm, something that distinguishes you, something other people lack. But collect enough deadwood and the spark leaves nothing but ash. That's where I am, full of ash and devoid of confidence. You need confidence to get a job, but you also need a job to gain confidence (causality thingy!). At this point, if I were to receive a callback for a job interview, I'd probably piss myself. Like an old murderer who suffers a heart attack on release from prison, unable to handle the change in status quo.

For the past three nights I've slept under a bridge. This has been an eye-opening experience. Down here, it's a close-knit society founded on misery. Yet down here is the best I've felt in years. Finally, I can breathe again. You're in a truly vulnerable position; desperation all around you. Sleep with one eye open and trust people you wouldn't so much as nod to in the upper world. It's all so eerily familiar.

I can't remember the last time I journaled. Thinking on my condition hasn't been a priority so much as basic hygiene. No one believes I'm homeless and sober. Even other homeless.

Everyone here seems to be afflicted with something beyond just the crippling doubt I can't seem to overcome. I could—in theory—start over and go back to being sad and trapped. I've been looking at cell tower jobs. Seems dangerous, and I imagine coworkers depend on one another. I've adapted to homeless life so well that I no longer recognize myself. This passed the ultimate test when I encountered my wife today. She must be a tourist in my new city. There was a part of me who wanted to say hi. I can imagine this mischievously and also tragically. "Guess who!" I might say. Or I might fall at her feet begging forgiveness. Someone from the upper world who would take me in, clean me up, and treat me like a human being—not the animal existence I seem to prefer. Instead, I pulled my hat down to hide my face. It's too embarrassing to let her see me this way.

Today she walked right by me. She has also reinvented herself. For the better, I'm pleased to report. New hairstyle. A cozy sweater suitable for this hip, wet town. She looks homey. Not like someone whose prestigious job is driving her nuts. More like someone ready to spend a summer camping, unconcerned that camping is a waste of valuable social-climbing time. I'm resting in my sleeping bag when she walks by. She must sense me in here because her pace slows. That's when I have in mind to reach for her taut jogger's ankle and grip sharply, reminiscent of the pranks we used to play when newly in love. Of course, that might result in a foot to the face.

She's not mine anymore, and I'm not hers.

I belong to no one.

Only a few pages left. I've thought a long time about how best to fill them. I've been waiting for something meaningful, and this is it. I've found God. Or God has found me (causality spiral!). I was sleeping in the bricked doorway of a Baptist church when it happened. This little old lady with a ball of white hair arrived at 0500 to begin prepping for Sunday services. I start to gather my things, and she welcomes me inside for a cup of coffee. The rest played out as clichély as a gospel movie. It was the first time in a long time someone from the upper world acknowledged my existence beyond slinking-away well-wishes. I didn't know how to behave.

"Shouldn't you be afraid of me?" I said.

"Why would I be afraid of someone who reminds me of my grandson," she fired back.

I didn't know whether to laugh or cry.

Why was it a Baptist church where I found God? Why not a mosque, a Hindu temple, or a Catholic diocese? Convenience, that's why. The church's side entrance is sheltered and warm, close enough to a major byway for a hasty escape. Though it wasn't so much the tradition as it was the person who welcomed me into it. Her name is Mary, naturally. I believe she's in her eighties.

I find it ironic the spine of this patriarchal religion is composed entirely of grandmas. That the most devoted early followers of Christ were mostly women. Jesus, with his instinctively feminine message of love and care for all, makes so little sense that I figure it must be true. And the military is already rife with cherry-picked Christian posturing. "No love is greater than he who takes a bullet to the dome for the reformed gangbanger suppressing fire by his side." But then Jesus says it's easy to love our own tribe—and not even that commendable. Even the grubbiest of society favors their clan. What about love for your enemy? Love for the Taliban. *Ha! Fuck those fucking fucks!* Still, I chewed on that line for a great while. Could I find it in my heart to at least pray for the

Taliban? Mystical messaging Gandhi, Lincoln, and MLK all took and ran with and used to change the world.

Here's what I believe:

A squirrel is born programmed to do squirrelly things, but no human is born knowing how to be a person. For that, we look to those around us and take on the various identity patterns we see in the hopes they're a good enough fit. For me, that identity was a soldier. It fit like Oakley gloves until I came home and no one could understand me unless I was damaged, as per their expectations. That's when I realized these pre-packaged identities are a trap we keep falling for, again and again and again. Don't get me wrong, it brings joy to my heart to see a kid trick-or-treating as Captain America, but Captain America is too one-dimensional to fully explain the nuances of human life. Captain America is a transitory phase. Fun for an evening, destructive to cling to when it's time to move on.

Thankfully, long ago, a man-God came and preached on a mountain the highest form of human behavior. Three rules:

Love your God

Love your Neighbor

Love the fucking Taliban

If you prioritize love, then you don't need shallow projections to be whole. You can learn to become whomever you want, so long as it's with a loving attitude, which naturally puts you in the best relation to others.

Now, people say these ancient stories have run their course. They're outmoded—antiquated—cannot be countenanced with modern life. A poor man's crutch, perhaps, but not much else. That might be true. But, brother, you wouldn't look at a man dragging a mangled and deformed foot and ask about his cane, would you?

"Excuse me, Sir, I think you would be better off without that. As you can see, I'm much faster relying on my own two feet."

Bully for that person. Not great for the man with the cane.

So it goes with my soul.

I don't know if I'll ever solve enough problems to feel self-worth again. I don't know if I have honeycombs scrambling my brain. I only know the words and deeds of a peasant-child born in a Middle East village, has renewed my heart and mind. Truly, this is the only relief I have ever known.

Of this I am certain.

ACKNOWLEDGMENTS

I would like to thank Phil Halton and the fine team at Double Dagger for taking a chance on this debut collection. Your kindness will not be forgotten.

A special thank you to Erika Salamonsen, who put up with me, sacrificed for me, and helped create a calm and focused environment for me to write these stories. This book would not exist without you.

Thank you, Courtney Brkic, who read the manuscript an ungodly number of times, responding with detailed feedback for each iteration.

My sincere appreciation to Christopher Lyke. Thank you for your time and your interest in my work. I hope I can return the favor one day.

I'd like to mention my mother and father, who have championed my stories since before I knew grammar.

Shout-out also to George Mason's MFA Fiction Family who provided much-needed friendship and feedback. I can't list you all, but you know who you are.

Fuck it, let's try and list you all:

Courtney Brkic, Tania James, Helon Habila, Alexia Arthurs, Timothy Johnson, Kevin Binder, Kat Colvert, Leah Sumrall, Frannie Dove, Miriam Gyimah, Jihoon Park, Izbit Siebel, Meagan Trammell, Phillip Spinella, Andrew Joseph White, Zachary Barnes, Delaney Burke, Bareerah Ghani, Kayla Hare, Michael Hock, Alex Horne, Julianne Iannone, Emilie Knudsen, Ivan Moore, Farheen Raparthi, DT Schatten, Tommy Sheffield, Erin Snyder, John Stohl, Asa Sutton, Grace Taber, Katelyn Steagall, Stephanie Runyon, Alice Baker, Arpita Roy, and Lizzie Terrell.

It was a pleasure learning and growing with you.

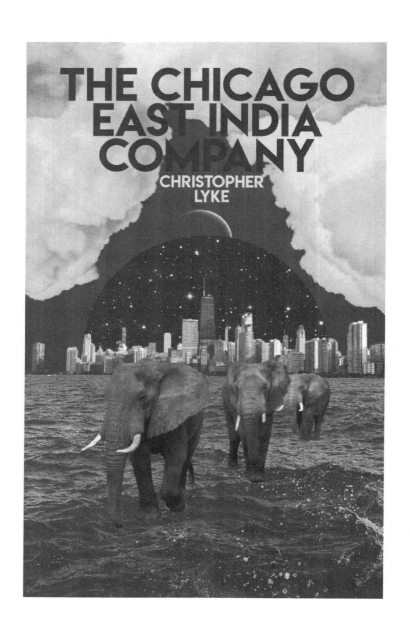

THE CHICAGO
EAST INDIA
COMPANY

CHRISTOPHER
LYKE

THE CHICAGO EAST INDIA COMPANY

No matter what we think we are achieving, eventually, imperial wars come home to roost. A generation of men asked to watch children suffer without flinching return to America. The ethics of the wars of Pax Americana become the ways and mores in our own streets. The logic of the war in Afghanistan is transferred to the classrooms of Chicago's public high schools. America is reborn in a shape we never intended.

A series of short stories and vignettes walk the reader through the consequences of two decades of war, and the attitudes it creates. Lyke's setting shifts in time and place but forever casts the main character of The Chicago East India Company as someone trying to maintain his sanity, his humanity, and his kindness as the state and its bureaucratic machinations unknowingly try to take them away.

In the tradition of Camus, Orwell or Steinbeck, Lyke's work illuminates human nature, and seeks the truth hidden under layers of grit.

ABOUT THE AUTHOR

Christopher Lyke is an American writer and teacher living in Chicago. He served in Afghanistan and Africa as an enlisted infantryman in the U.S. Army. Chris co-founded and edits Line of Advance, a literary blog for veterans, as well as overseeing the annual Colonel Darron L. Wright Memorial Writing Awards. He can usually be found running with his dog in Logan Square or catching a game at Floyd's Pub.

11/3/11

9/11 was an inside job.

The moon landings were faked.

JFK is alive and well and spends his days with Elvis.

Everyone knows what happened on 11/3/11. But do they really know the truth?

John Doe – JD to his friends – knows for a fact that things are not as they seem. The world is wearing blinders, but he has his eyes wide open. And the more you truly know, the crazier you seem.

Dive into a rabbit hole of conspiracy theories and see the world through JD's eyes. AE Merrick's debut novel is a wild ride through mind control, paranoia, and isolation in search of the ever-elusive truth.

ABOUT THE AUTHOR

A.E. Merrick is a Toronto-based dilettante who has experimented with a number of different identities, occupations, and pastimes. They are uncomfortable with publicly searchable databases of personal information. They write truth rather than fiction. 11/3/11 is their first novel.

DOUBLE†DAGGER

— www.doubledagger.ca —

Double Dagger Books is Canada's only military-focused publisher. Conflict and warfare have shaped human history since before we began to record it. The earliest stories that we know of, passed on as oral tradition, speak of war, and more importantly, the essential elements of the human condition that are revealed under its pressure. We are dedicated to publishing material that, while rooted in conflict, transcends the idea of "war" as merely a genre. Fiction, non- fiction, and stuff that defies categorization, we want to read it all.

Because if you want peace, study war.

ABOUT THE AUTHOR

A Purple Heart recipient, Benjamin served three years in the Army and has worked an odd array of jobs—private investigator, personal trainer, peer support at a crisis receiving center. So far, the highlight of his résumé was teaching literature as a grad student at George Mason University.

Follow him on Instagram @Inks__Thinks

Made in the USA
Middletown, DE
25 August 2023